Quinn's Last Run

The stage to Yuma was down and the Jicarilla Apaches were attacking. The driver had been killed and only Tom Quinn now stood between the renegades and the young blonde woman travelling with him.

The arrival of Sheriff Mike Hancock appears to ease the crisis but, in fact, complicates matters even further. Hancock is escorting a murderer to Yuma Prison and now Quinn must take him aboard the coach as well.

Pressed into service, Quinn must drive the stagecoach across a hundred miles of dangerous country, rife with Indians, infested by border raiders and complicated by the arrival of one particular passenger.

This is no way to begin a career as a stage driver, and the question hovers ominously – is this to be Quinn's first run or his last?

Quinn's Last Run

Owen G. Irons

A Black Horse Western

ROBERT HALE · LONDON

© Owen G. Irons 2010
First published in Great Britain 2010

ISBN 978-0-7090-8827-1

Robert Hale Limited
Clerkenwell House
Clerkenwell Green
London EC1R 0HT

www.halebooks.com

Typeset by
Derek Doyle & Associates, Shaw Heath
Printed and bound in Great Britain by
CPI Antony Rowe, Chippenham and Eastbourne

ONE

At this late hour the brooding purple-shot clouds above the Arizona desert were as foreboding as midnight on the twelfth of Never. Pushed up all the way from the Gulf of Mexico in front of a waning hurricane, they had crossed the Mexican heartland and entered US territory like some uncertain invading army. From time to time it would rain just enough to pock the sandy soil. Now and again the wind would increase as if the storm were trying to gather bluster, but right now it was hot, dark and still across the long desert.

Jody Short was thinking that the winds would tear the fabric of the clouds apart long before they reached Yuma Territorial Prison. It would likely be a clear, white day in the walled courtyard when they hanged him in front of two guards, who would be assigned as witnesses to the execution and asked to sign his death certificate.

He supposed he had been a hardcase, a troublemaker for most of his short life, but as far as killing the woman. . . .

'I didn't do it, Hancock!' he shouted out in frustration. His companion, the man with the badge on his shirt, did not even turn his head, but continued leading Jody's horse onward.

'I told you before, Short, I'm not a judge.'

'I'm telling you—'

'Won't do you a bit of good to tell me,' Mike Hancock grumbled. 'Someone sure as hell killed Dolores Delgado, and there are witnesses willing to testify that it was you.'

'They're wrong, I swear it! Or else they're lying,' Jody said in frustration. Hancock did not answer. The lawman continued to sit his plodding gray horse, the rope stretched between them tied to his saddle horn and the reins of Jody Short's buckskin pony.

They moved across flat desert, passing stands of shaggy Joshua trees and giant saguaro cactus.

'When are we going to stop, Hancock? I've about had it. My horse is in bad shape, too.'

'Not out here,' the lawman replied, still not turning his head. 'I've got my schedule to keep. We should make Las Palmas in a little over an hour.'

'At least we can find some beans and tortillas there,' Jody Short muttered. 'You don't even let a man eat.'

'You won't have to worry about that before long, will you? But listen, Short,' Hancock said, now swiveling in his saddle to look back at the young outlaw, 'when we get to Las Palmas, be careful what you say. If they find out that you murdered that Mexican woman, what they'll do to you would make you pray that you had met the hangman in Yuma.'

'What do they have to do with it? Even if it were true that I killed Dolores. We're on this side of the border, aren't we? Not in Mexico.'

'That's right,' Hancock answered, 'but some of these border people have difficulty making that distinction. Just keep your mouth shut.'

'All right, I . . . what in hell is that?' Jody said abruptly, standing in his stirrups. Hancock frowned, slipped his Winchester from its saddle scabbard and slowed his horse, staring across the darkness of the clouded night desert.

'We'd better see,' Hancock said in a low voice. He had drawn his horse to a halt now, glancing across his shoulder to make sure his manacled prisoner had remained at the full length of the tethering rope. 'Come on.'

He started his gray horse again, walking it toward the dark bulk of the object lying beside the road. A horse nickered and then another. Nearing the dark object, Hancock could now make out the familiar shape of a stagecoach, although it was turned on its side. The horses, still in their twisted harness, stamped the ground with impatient anger.

'Is someone there?' Hancock called out, levering a .44-40 cartridge into the breech of his Winchester.

'Who's asking?'

'Marshal Mike Hancock out of Yuma.'

'Mike?' A man rose from behind the overturned coach and waved a hand. 'It's me, Tom Quinn.'

'Quinn? I'll be damned. What happened, did you hit a rut?'

'I wish that had been all,' Quinn said, appearing around the back wheel of the stagecoach to stride toward Hancock. He was a tall, well-set-up man with dark hair and a torn blue shirt. He shot an appraising glance in Jody Short's direction.

'One for Yuma Prison?' Quinn asked.

'Yeah. What happened here, Quinn?'

'A band of Apaches. I think they were Jicarillas. They jumped us about a mile back. Tank Dawson was driving. I tried to fight them off.'

'How many were there?' Jody Short asked with excitement.

'Fifteen or so. Anyway, they got Dawson and I took it into my head that I could manage the team and shoot back at the same time. As you can see, that didn't work out real well.'

Both marshal and prisoner had stepped down from their horses now, Short, in manacles, dismounting clumsily.

'Fifteen Apaches?' Jody Short said with doubt in his voice as the three men walked to the far side of the fallen stage. 'I don't hardly believe it. One man against all those savages. It can't be. How?' he wanted to know.

In the dim light Mike Hancock could see Tom Quinn's expression tighten. Quinn's reply, though he felt obliged to give none, was to toe a cardboard box resting on the sand behind the coach. Hancock recognized it for what it was – a box meant to contain fifty Winchester cartridges. As the box tipped on to its side a single brass .44 rolled from it.

'That box was full when I started firing,' Quinn said. Quickly he changed the subject. 'There are two wounded passengers just off the road. Maybe we can help them.'

One of these was sitting up now, holding his head and groaning. A portly, partly bald man in a blue suit. The other was a young woman with light-brown hair.

She lay flat on her back beneath a striped blanket. She opened her eyes as they approached and the thinning clouds parted enough for them to catch starlight and reflect it. Quinn crouched down and felt her forehead.

'How bad's she hurt?' Mike Hancock asked. Even in the dim light it was plain that she was a beautiful young thing.

'I don't know,' Quinn said. 'She was knocked out, that's for sure. As far as internal injuries, who knows?'

The portly man, who had been sitting rubbing his head, now looked at them and demanded in an obnoxious tone of voice: 'When are we going to get moving? I'm George Sabato! I've business to take care of. What are you going to do about getting us rolling?'

Other than glancing his way, the others ignored him.

'I don't think it will take a lot to upright the coach,' Quinn was saying. 'You've got a rope. Toss it up and over and we'll tie it on. Your horse can supply most of the muscle. The other two of us can shove up from this side once it starts to lift.'

'I'm cuffed,' Jody Short complained, holding up his manacled hands.

'You can push just as well that way,' Quinn said.

That was the way they did it. Mike Hancock tied the rope on across the doorjamb between the two windows, tossed the rope across the stage and mounted his gray horse. As he rode it slowly forward the rope grew taut and the side of the stagecoach away from the wheels began to lift from the ground. When there were a few inches to slip their hands underneath Quinn and an unhappy Jody Short hoisted the carriage-works upward. It was only a matter of a few minutes' work to upright the coach. Quinn inspected front and rear axles and pronounced them sound.

'Any of those horses lame?' Mike asked from horseback, nodding toward the coach team.

'I don't think so. Check them over will you, Mike? Then come back and help me lift the lady into the coach.'

'I'll help you,' George Sabato said, but watching him now, Quinn could see the man was still wobbly from the fall he had taken.

'That's all right, Mr Sabato,' Quinn said. 'Just climb aboard yourself. We'll soon have you on your way.'

'All right,' Sabato said, still rubbing at the front of his balding head. 'I'm sorry about the way I spoke before. I took a harder knock than I thought.'

'That's all right,' Quinn answered. 'Don't give it another thought. We've all had a rough trip.'

Heavily the fat man climbed aboard the coach. Jody Short beside Quinn asked: 'What about me? Do I get on?'

'That's between you and Mike Hancock,' Quinn replied. 'He may prefer to ride on alone with you.'

Hancock had been considering the point as he checked out the stagecoach team. Returning now, he told Quinn: 'They seem to be in good enough shape. The off-wheel horse might have been nicked by a bullet along its flank – hard to tell in this light.'

'What about him,' Quinn asked, jerking his head toward Jody Short. 'Want to let him ride in the coach or not?'

'I suppose so,' Hancock said wearily. 'As long as he's wearing those manacles I guess it's safe enough. Our own horses are kind of beat down, Quinn. Probably better to get our weight off their backs. At least as far as Las Palmas. I'll consider matters again after we reach the town.'

'All right then,' Quinn said. 'I'll drive, you ride shotgun, if that suits you.'

'It'll have to,' Hancock said with a laugh. 'I've never handled a four-horse team.'

'I don't claim to be a professional at it myself,' Quinn answered with a smile, 'but I did pick up a few pointers from Tank Dawson along the trail. There was a man who could drive 'em. The horses knew his touch on the reins.'

'I guess we'd better get started,' Mike Hancock said with some uneasiness now as he studied the long desert. Would the Apaches return? There was no telling.

'I guess we had,' Quinn agreed. 'Give me a hand with the woman.'

Working swiftly but gently, they were able to get the lady up into the coach, laying her down on the

13

rear-facing seat. George Sabato leaned against the wall beside the opposite seat. Jody Short sat slumped beside him. Hancock checked his manacles and reminded him:

'There's nowhere to run to out here, Short.'

Quinn lingered near the woman for a moment. He folded a spare blanket for a pillow and placed it under her head. He covered her with the striped blanket and studied her face again. Straight nose, full mouth, cheeks a little gaunted from the long trail, light-brown hair loose across her shoulders. There was a smudge of dirt on her temple and what looked to be the beginnings of a bruise. Twenty, was she? Twenty-five? Young anyway. She had never explained what she was doing out here alone.

'Quinn?' Mike Hancock said, nudging Quinn out of his reverie. 'Help me with the two saddle horses. We'll slip their gear and tie them on behind.'

'All right,' Quinn said impatiently. He backed away from the girl, stepped down and closed the stage door. He was irritated, not at Hancock's reasonable request, but with himself for wasting time watching the woman. There was no time to be wasted musing over her. Not if they wanted to get off the desert alive.

At last, with the horses Jody Short and Marshal Hancock had been riding tied on behind, their saddles tossed up to ride on the roof, Quinn stepped up on to the bench seat of the stagecoach, gathered the multiple leather ribbons guiding the team, used his boot to release the brake and started the team forward toward Las Palmas. Hancock sat at his side, rifle in hand, eyes alert to each shadow cast by dune or cactus, rock or ridge.

'How far?' Mike called out as the stage rolled on, dust streaming out behind it.

'I'm guessing no more than an hour,' Quinn called back. Then he muttered a small curse. The team was balky for some reason. He thought that Mike had been correct about the off-wheel lead horse. It probably was wounded. It kept trying to pull away from the harnesses, to bolt free, and the other three horses resented it. Quinn adjusted the handling of the reins he held in his leather gloved hands just slightly, trying to accommodate the wounded horse. Tank Dawson would have known how to handle the team; Quinn did not.

'I'm going to have to slow them down some,' Quinn said.

'You're the driver,' Hancock replied. 'We aren't going to outrun any raiding party anyway.'

'I guess not,' Quinn said, tugging back slightly on the reins. 'The Indians were all mounted. I don't think I've ever heard of that many Apaches choosing to fight from horseback.'

'No. They prefer to fight afoot. Seems to me that with all those horses, they were planning on covering some ground in a hurry. Army after them, maybe. I'd guess they just happened to run across the stage and decided to take the horses . . . and maybe a few scalps.'

'It's a good guess,' Quinn conceded. 'In time they would have overrun me. I think they pulled out not because of my rifle but because they had something more important in mind.'

After another mile or so, jolting over uneven ground, Mike asked: 'That woman back there, what's she doing way out here alone? For that matter, Quinn, what are you doing on a stagecoach?'

'I don't know anything about the girl,' Quinn said, slowing the team to guide it into and up out of a dry wash. 'She didn't have much to say – or maybe it was just that she didn't want to talk to me,' he added with a short laugh.

He went on: 'I was on my way down to Carrizo – you know where that is? Not far from Nogales. A man there had a string of horses that I was looking to buy. You know where my place is, right? I've got good graze for a lot of horses up in those hills, but stock is hard to come by.'

'What happened?' Mike asked as they hit the flats again. Now, far ahead, the lawman thought he could see a string of lights blinking across the distance. Las Palmas; or so he dearly hoped.

Tom Quinn continued: 'By the time I got to Carrizo the rancher had been burned out. Border raiders. They had taken the herd and driven it across into Mexico, I guess. My own pony was pretty beat up by then, and I was tired of the saddle myself so I rode into Carrizo, sold the pony, and bought myself a stagecoach ticket back.'

'I see. Tough, isn't it, the way plans can go bad?'

'Out here,' Quinn said, gesturing with a gloved hand, 'if you can get one plan out of ten to work out, you're doing fine.'

Yes, Hancock thought, the long desert had a way of ruining plans – and breaking men.

The twinkling lights in the distance seemed to be growing nearer. 'I think that's Las Palmas,'

17

Hancock said with a nod.

'Let's hope so.'

'The border raiders who stole that horse herd, that wouldn't have been our old friend, Guerrero and his bunch, would it?' Mike asked.

'I've no idea. I heard that he was locked up over in Riodoso, but they could have busted him out of jail, I suppose. If it was Guerrero, he made a mistake passing up this coach down in Carrizo in favor of a string of horses, no matter how good they were.'

'I don't get you,' Hancock said frowning in puzzlement.

'This stage is carrying a little something extra, Mike. In the boot there's twenty thousand dollars in gold heading for Yuma Prison to pay the guards, feed the prisoners and maintain the facility.'

'Holy. . . ! And you don't think that's the reason the Apaches hit it?'

'If so, they gave up awfully easy. Besides, Mike, you know as well as I do that an Apache has little use for gold. He can't ride into a town and buy whatever he likes. They're a nomadic people; they don't have artisans who can sit in one place long enough to make jewelry or golden idols like those Indians deeper down in Mexico used to. It's shiny and appealing, but it's heavy enough that it's inconvenient to tote around from place to place. No, Mike, they just wanted the horses and then decided that they just weren't worth the trouble.

'It's not anything I'm going to worry about now, either,' Quinn continued. 'In Las Palmas I'm delivering the coach to the stage office, slapping the dust from my jeans, buying another horse and riding home. Let them worry about the gold. It's none of my concern.'

The stage hit a deep rut and bounced into the air a few inches. Quinn slowed the horses still more. They were weary and now the pueblo of Las Palmas could be seen ahead clearly. Quinn said to Mike Hancock:

'I hope that the girl is riding comfortably. That bump was enough to send her rolling to the floor.'

'There's two men back there to make sure that doesn't happen,' the lawman replied.

'Yes, you're right, of course. But does George Sabato strike you as a man to be counted on in any circumstance?'

Hancock smiled thinly and shook his head. 'No, no, I can't say that he does.'

19

'Well, there's your prisoner. He can brace her up even wearing manacles. What is Jody Short, Mike? A cattle rustler or something?'

'No,' Mike Hancock had to tell Quinn. 'He murdered a woman.'

TWO

It was the middle of the night before they rolled into Las Palmas. The skies were clearer, but the air was heavy and humid. Quinn's shirt was pasted to his chest with perspiration. The street they rolled into was quiet, deserted.

'Any idea where the stage station is?' Quinn asked the lawman.

'No. It's probably on this street though, it only makes sense. We'll find it.'

Fortunately the horses had a better idea of where they were going than Quinn and Hancock did. Sensing water, hay and a rubdown, they strained against the reins. Quinn let them have their heads.

Halfway along the street, which was flanked with

21

low adobe-block buildings, they came upon the stage depot. A light burned within and a sign hanging on hooks and rings from the awning proved that they had stumbled upon the stagecoach station.

A bulky man with a florid face and thinning red hair appeared on the porch in front of the depot, frowned in their direction and then stalked to the halted coach.

'Where in hell is Dawson, and who in the hell are you?' he demanded.

'Tank's dead. We had Apache trouble.'

'That figures,' the big man answered, as if all the world's troubles were bound to come his way.

'As for who we are, we'll discuss matters with you after we climb down. Is there someone around to tend to the team?'

'I'll rouse the hostler – he's sleeping. He'll be plenty mad. Coach is five hours late.'

'Couldn't be helped,' Quinn said. He looped the reins around the brake handle and stepped down, followed by Mike Hancock.

The door to the stagecoach had swung open and now George Sabato stood stretching his back, looking around at the desolate little town.

'We've got an injured woman inside,' Quinn

told the big man, who seemed to be the station manager. 'Have you a bed we can take her to?'

'Yes, of course.' His face now reflected more concern than anger. 'Need any help with her?'

'No, sir. Thank you but we can manage.'

'All right, better come along inside.'

Jody Short had now emerged from the stage, clearly manacled.

'Who is that?' the station manager asked unhappily,

'My prisoner,' Hancock said, tapping his badge which had not been visible before.

'I see. It's going to be one of those nights, is it? Let me get the door open and I'll call my wife to see to the woman's needs.'

'Mike,' Quinn said in a low voice, 'do you think that you and Sabato there can handle carrying the girl inside?'

'Why, aren't you. . . ? Oh, I see,' Mike said understanding. One of them would have to see to the gold, and Hancock needed to keep watch over his prisoner at the same time. 'All right.' To Jody Short he said, 'We're going inside now, Short. You're going to sit down in the first chair you see, and you're going to stay there.'

Quinn stood watching in the night as Jody Short

was herded into the low adobe structure and Mike and George Sabato returned to help the injured young woman from the coach. She was able to stand on her own feet now in a wobbly fashion. That alone was encouraging. The station manager must have gone to rouse the hostler from his sleep, for from some unseen building behind the station a string of oaths stained the quiet solitude of the night. Quinn smiled and went to the boot of the coach.

Untying the fastenings on the leather covered boot, he searched for and found the heavy canvas sack with the leather grips. He was dragging the gold from there when he heard a pistol cock behind him and a near-at-hand voice hiss.

'Get your hands off of that, Quinn.'

The voice was recognizable as George Sabato's. Quinn turned slowly to see Sabato, hatless, standing there with a Remington .36 revolver pointed at him.

'I never took you for a thief, Quinn,' the fat man said.

'I'm not. I'm just removing these goods before the coach is led away to the stable. What makes it your business anyway, Sabato?'

'What?' the round-faced man said, taking

another step closer. 'I am an employee of the Territorial Penitentiary at Yuma. A guard there for twenty-three years. That . . . those goods were placed under my protection.'

'Fine,' Quinn said, turning away. 'Protect them.'

With that he dropped the canvas bag and strode away toward the open door to the lighted stage office. He cared nothing about Sabato and his problems, nothing about the gold. It would have helped if the fat man had identified himself earlier as a prison official, but it did not matter. He was through with the gold, through with the stagecoach, through with. . . .

The young woman with the developing bruise on her forehead was sitting up in an overstuffed chair near the low-burning fireplace, sipping coffee or tea from a tiny cup. Her gaze flickered briefly toward Quinn's eyes and fell away again.

Quinn stood silently staring at the crimson and gold of the fire burning in the stone hearth until, minutes later, they were called to dinner at the long plank table in an inner room. The stage station master – introduced as Aaron Pyle – sat at the head of the table. His wife served platters of meat and potatoes. She was a tiny creature with Spanish eyes that seemed constantly fearful.

Quinn noticed this as he noticed other events going on around him: Jody Short struggling to eat with manacled hands, Mike Hancock's apparent weariness, the concerned expression on the face of the lady passenger, the hasty eating by George Sabato, who accompanied his meal with grunts of appreciation.

He watched all of this, but none of it had any real relevance. He finished half of his meal, rose and left the room with only a nod of thanks to Pyle's Mexican wife. He wanted nothing to do with these people. Mike Hancock, of course, he knew from his backtrail, but he and Mike had never been close friends in any sense. When Hancock had been pursuing Ernesto Guerrero up along the Yavapai, Quinn had reluctantly pinned on a deputy marshal's badge. Guerrero had been taking stock – horses and cattle – from the ranchers around Quinn's spread and driving them to Mexico.

They never caught up with Guerrero, although they had taken a small toll on his gang.

Nearly a year later Guerrero had been arrested in Riodoso, ending his career as a border raider. Quinn had worked with Mike Hancock, but had never gotten close to the marshal.

As for considering the girl – she seemed to be all right now, was eating healthily. And he had taken offense at George Sabato's manner when Quinn had been trying only to help. He had no interest in Sabato's problems either. He wanted only to get home once again.

All Quinn wanted to do now was catch a night's sleep, purchase a horse in the morning and strike out for his ranch. He appreciated the problems of the others, but it was hardly his obligation to aid them. He had brought the stage through to Las Palmas – not that any of them had thanked him for it – but that had been as much for himself as for them. Now let them fend for themselves.

Quinn stepped out on to the porch in front of the low adobe building and stood studying the silent town, the starry skies. He first caught a breath of some flowery scent and then heard the rustle of skirts as the young woman from the stagecoach slipped up beside him to lean her hands on the railing and look skyward herself.

'I am Lily Davenport,' she said without looking directly at Quinn.

'Glad to know you,' Quinn answered carefully.

'I wanted to thank you for what you did back there.'

'It's all right.'

'What will you do now?' she asked, suddenly focusing her shining eyes on his.

'Do? I'm going home, Lily Davenport.'

'To. . . ?'

'A little place I've built up in the Yavapai Valley. There are people, obligations waiting for me.'

'But can't you. . . ? I heard the men talking,' she continued, still hesitantly. What was she driving at?

'What about?' he asked carefully. She had stepped nearer to him, and yes she was young and beautiful, her body slender, compactly arranged.

'There's no driver!' she said with a sudden burst of emotion. Her hand reached for his shirt sleeve and then fell away. 'This man, Tank Dawson, was supposed to rest here for the night and then drive the stage the rest of the way into Yuma.'

'They'll find somebody to take you,' Quinn answered.

'But . . . what if there is no one? I must be in Yuma tomorrow.' Now she did touch his arm lightly. Quinn smiled at her and then shook his head. 'Looks like you will be late in that case. They'll have to send for another driver.'

'But you—'

Quinn interrupted her. 'But I am not a

stagecoach driver, never wanted to be, only wish to get home and take care of my own business.'

She looked up at him, tried a smile, let it fall away and said sharply, 'I did not think that you were a cruel man!'

That said, she hoisted her skirts and stalked back into the stage stop, leaving Quinn to watch her rigid back.

'What did you do to offend the lady?' Mike Hancock asked as he stepped out to join Quinn at the rail.

'Nothing,' Quinn said, returning Mike's smile. 'She wanted something done her way and I told her it wasn't my way.'

'One of those, huh?' Mike mused. 'I came out to tell you that the lady of the house is saving some dessert for you – blackberry cobbler and coffee.'

'Have you any idea,' Quinn asked, ignoring the invitation, 'where a man can find a decent horse and tack in this town?'

'I've never been through here but once,' Hancock answered, 'and that was years ago. Ask Pyle. The station master must know. Maybe he's even got a spare saddle horse himself. Now, why don't you come in and try that cobbler? I noticed you didn't eat but half of your supper.'

'I don't think I want any, Mike.'

'Why? No sweet tooth?'

Quinn was bluntly honest. 'I don't want to look at George Sabato across the table. I'm not crazy about Lily Davenport. Jody Short – I felt like I had to keep my eyes on him all through supper, waiting for him to make a move. I just don't think dessert would be good for my digestion.'

'Do as you like.' Mike shrugged, stepping away from the rail. 'It's your stomach. Me, I've been on trail rations for three days. I'm going to eat first and worry about my digestion later.'

Thinking about what he was missing made Quinn's stomach grumble just a little, but as he had told Mike, he did not care to eat with those people. He decided to take a short walk uptown. Perhaps he would be able to find a stable where a horse could be purchased.

There was an unhappy feeling surrounding this group. Some sort of unidentifiable dark aura. He had no sympathy for any of them. Jody Short, an accused woman killer, Sabato with his quick gun and accusing eyes guarding the gold, Lily Davenport with her twitch of indignation after not getting her way. He walked the sandy streets, searching for more companionable people.

There was a cantina open. A narrow, squat adobe, its face splashed with the red white and green of Mexico's national colors, but, glancing in, Quinn saw no other pale faces and he decided not to enter. No matter what people said, believed (or pretended to), outsiders are not always welcome.

No matter, he was not thirsty for alcohol and so he walked on, glancing now and then at the ragged, wind-torn clouds overhead. The stars were bright in the gaps of the clouds, dancing in a night sky that was nearly black. The storm had broken. Morning would dawn clear and the way to his ranch along the Yavapai would be over dry ground.

And he was ready to start for home. There would be time for taking care of his stomach once the ranch was reached.

The voice from the alley said 'Hey!' as Quinn passed, and he halted, looking curiously into its shadowed depths.

'Me?' he asked.

'Yes, you.'

Puzzled, Quinn stood uncertainly at the head of the alley. He frowned, not responding. It was not a clever idea to step into a dark, narrow alley where a stranger beckoned.

It was then that they jumped him from behind.

31

There were two of them, Quinn thought, perhaps more, but they were at least three as the man who had called to him rushed to join in the assault, The sheer weight of their bodies drove Quinn to the earth. He swung out wildly, but had no real chance of driving them off. The fists and boots of his attackers slammed into his legs, his ribs. The men unleashed each blow with grunts of effort, giving him their best shots.

Quinn could not rise. Two of them were now sitting on him. A heavy blow to his jaw sent his head reeling, the stars created by the blow were brighter than the desert stars, more colorful. He just gave up the fight. With legs and arms pinned down, with hundreds of pounds of sweating male flesh on top of him there was no chance at all to fight free.

He felt one man rise and then another. A last kick was delivered to his back, just above his kidney. A voice from the darkness growled.

'We know who you are, driver. You're not going to take that stagecoach out of Las Palmas in the morning. Do you understand!'

'I understand,' Quinn said, breathing heavily. 'I won't.'

'If you do . . . this is just a hint of what could

happen to you, driver,' one of them said. He was only a featureless, shadowed figure hovering over Tom Quinn. 'Remember that you were warned.'

Then they trudged away, leaving Tom Quinn alone and hurting in the cold, dirty alley.

It was a long time before Quinn was able to rise. The alley was dark and empty. There were no sounds to be heard across all of Las Palmas. Struggling to his feet he staggered a little and was forced to lean against the wall of a building for support. His back hurt, his ribs hurt, his head ached and throbbed.

All over nothing. He did not know the men who had attacked him, had done nothing to them, had had no intention of driving the stagecoach on in the morning.

Not until then. Now he stooped, retrieved his revolver and with a perverse sort of consideration thought things over. The why of matters he could not even guess at. He just did not like people trying to beat him into a certain way of thinking. Perhaps he should show the men that they had achieved the exact opposite of their objective. It would prove nothing to anyone except himself, but he considered. Maybe he would continue on to Yuma.

He did not feel that he owed it to the stage line, to George Sabato, certainly not to the stormy little Lily Davenport. Nor even to the fallen Tank Dawson who would never complete his last run.

It was something he would have to think through over the course of the long night. Just now he planted his hat back on his head and, holding his ribs, he staggered his way along the empty street toward the stage station beneath the cold and lonely skies.

THREE

Marshal Mike Hancock sat across the low-ceilinged room from the fireplace where the logs burned, giving off warmth but little smoke. He had a serape folded as a lap robe over his arthritic knees. Pyle had provided Hancock with two shots of whiskey followed now by a mug of dark, bitter coffee. Mike found himself envying Aaron Pyle who spent all of his evenings like this, with an attentive little wife catering to him. And, not for the first time, he wondered why he had chosen his own way of life.

He was too old to be chasing outlaws and thieves across the badlands. There were mornings when just swinging into the saddle was a labor. The long rides across the sand dune country, over the waterless broken ground, had once seemed much easier. Now they were torture. If he thought he could afford to, perhaps find a situation like Aaron Pyle's, he would turn in his badge. It was a thought – perhaps Jody Short would be his last prisoner.

Short sat across the room, nearer to the native stone fireplace, shackled hands between his knees. He had managed to strike up a conversation, which Hancock could not hear, with Lily Davenport. The young woman was leaning forward in her chair, listening intently to whatever it was Jody was saying. The firelight made her eyes sparkle just as the starlight had earlier. She seemed recovered now. There was a bruise on her forehead, but with her hair now brushed, her face scrubbed, she was a remarkably striking woman. Hancock continued to watch them through half-lowered eyelids. His rifle still rested on his lap.

Because, you just never knew.

'So,' Jody Short was saying, 'they just placed the blame on me because I was in the area and they were too lazy to track down the real killer. I had never even met this Dolores Delgado, but they felt like they had to find someone guilty, and they chose me because I was unimportant, a man with no influence, of no standing. I was, simply, railroaded to clear their desks of the inquiry.'

'It must have been terrible for you,' Lily said with sympathy. She briefly touched the young man's knee, then drew her hand away.

'It'll be worse for me in Yuma when they stretch my neck,' Jody said, and his eyes seemed to moisten. 'For something I never did!' He raised his voice intentionally, so that Mike Hancock looked that way. Then Jody leaned back in his chair. 'There's no way out for me now.'

'Maybe someone will come forward,' Lily suggested. 'After a while.'

'They don't wait long in Yuma to hang you,' Jody responded bitterly. 'Besides, I doubt there were any witnesses. It's a long, empty land. The girl should have known better than to go out riding on her own.'

The eyes of all shifted as the front door opened and Tom Quinn entered. He moved heavily and was slightly bent over, holding his side.

Mike Hancock rose from his chair with concern. 'What happened, Quinn!'

'A little scuffle. Where's Pyle? I need a bed.'

Within minutes Quinn had been ushered into a tiny room with a cot and a high, narrow window. He managed to get his boots off, but only just, before he gave it up and lay down on his back to stare at the ceiling and watch the half-dozen visible stars through the window. He felt rotten. He was growing angrier, but hadn't the energy to sustain the anger while his body ached as it did.

Sleep was long in coming and when it did come it was fitful, incomplete. Tom Quinn had a lot of time to consider events.

When the first faint reddish hue filled the narrow window of his chamber Tom rose to sit on the side of the bunk. He was stiff, still weary and uncertain. The light of morning had not awakened him, and there had been no knock on the door. But from somewhere beyond the room he could smell eggs being cooked, tortillas warming, rich salsa and above all the scent of coffee. He struggled to put his boots on, pondering matters as he did so.

His night thoughts had done nothing to clarify matters. He reviewed what he knew and what he did not know. Someone did not want the coach to get through to Yuma. Who, why, was an enigma. Lily Davenport, that sleek haughty woman absolutely wanted the coach to roll on. She had told him that her journey was an urgent one. Why that might be, she had not indicated. George Sabato certainly wanted the stage to reach Yuma so that he could deliver the gold to the prison authorities. Jody Short, of course, did not. No man rushed toward his own hanging.

Who were the men who had jumped him last night? What did they want? There were several possibilities that came to mind. Perhaps they knew about the gold and did not want it transported farther.

Or . . . Quinn rose and ran his fingers through his hair before reaching for his hat. Or, perhaps it had been friends of Jody Short, planning on freeing him. Conversely, they could have been men who had known Dolores Delgado and wished to take Short to deal with him personally. If Lily Davenport. . . .

It was too much to think of with a throbbing head and an empty stomach. He swung the door wide and tramped down the short corridor to the kitchen where already the others, save Mike Hancock, were settled around the table. In front of them was a platterful of scrambled eggs, bowls of thick chunky salsa, fresh tortillas and a half-gallon-sized blue enamel pot filled with dark, strong coffee. Quinn slid on to the bench at the end of the table and was served almost immediately by Pyle's small, worried-appearing wife. He nodded his thanks, looked across the plank table at Lily Davenport whose mouth remained tight even as she ate.

'Where's Mike Hancock?' Quinn asked Aaron Pyle when he emerged from some back room, drying his hands on a small towel.

'He was here,' Pyle shrugged. 'I don't know.'

It wasn't like Mike to leave his prisoner unattended, even one in manacles.

'Maybe he felt sick,' George Sabato said. From the way the fat man was shoveling food into his mouth, he was feeling anything but ill.

'I'd better check on him,' Quinn said. No one answered. He folded his napkin, placed it aside and with his cup of coffee in hand started toward the front room of the stage station.

In one corner Mike Hancock sat sagged in a leather-strap chair, his rifle across his lap. He glanced up as Quinn approached across the room. 'Better eat up, Mike,' Quinn said, crouching down beside the marshal.

'So now *you*'re telling me?' Mike laughed. His color was not good; his eyes had a dull sheen.

'There's a long road ahead still,' Quinn said. 'You'll need your strength.'

'That's just it, Tom, my strength is gone. I left it

back on the long trail. When, where I don't know, but I'm feeling tired, shaky and suddenly old. I was thinking matters over last night, Tom.' Mike Hancock told him, 'I believe this is my last run. I am going to find another line of work. But I have to get the kid to Yuma Prison first! I won't end my career with a failure on my record.

'Tom,' Hancock asked, fixing pleading eyes on Quinn, 'would you reconsider driving the stagecoach the rest of the way? Riding aboard, with you there to help me watch the kid, I could make it.'

Tom said nothing. His perverse reaction to the beating he had taken the night before had been a hastily reached decision. In the morning light it had seemed only impulsive contrariness. He did not want to drive the stage. Why should he? Now looking at Mike Hancock's hopeful eyes he thought matters over again.

He had promised Tank that he would get the stage through – to Las Palmas – but there was no one there to finish Tank's last run for him. Now Mike Hancock, obviously weary and needing help, had asked him for the same favor.

Hell, what could another day out of his life cost him? The little ranch along the Yavapai would still be there when he reached it.

'All right, Mike,' Quinn said at length, rising out of his crouch. 'I'll help you make your last run.'

He returned to the kitchen where the others were finishing their meals. Sabato was dabbing elaborately at his thick lips with a blue napkin. There was salsa on his shirt-front. Lily Davenport, her plate pushed aside, sipped at her coffee. Jody Short wore a kind of contented sneer.

'How's the marshal?' the kid asked.

'Just fine,' Quinn answered coldly. 'Pyle,' he said to the station master, 'don't bother to send for another driver. I'll take the stage through to Yuma.'

Lily Davenport's eyes lit up and beamed her pleasure his way. Perhaps she had the mistaken idea that her charms had turned the trick. Sabato wore a toothy smile and for a moment Quinn feared that the government man was going to slap his shoulder with relief. In the end Sabato just murmured, 'Fine, fine!' Jody Short sat watching him without expression. Maybe he had hoped that somehow he could make his escape with the stage delayed and Mike Hancock ailing. Or maybe he was waiting for friends out there to arrive and help him. His eyes gave nothing away. His sullen mouth altered into a boyish smile which he directed at Lily Davenport.

'Well, miss, it looks like I'm going to be in your company for a little while.'

'Is the hostler up?' Quinn said, ignoring all of the by-play. Aaron Pyle nodded. Quinn suggested: 'Let's get that team hitched then. And you'd better have him tether the two saddle horses on behind.'

'Sure. Glad to,' Pyle said, relieved that he had averted any blame that might have been attributed to him for a delay of the coach's arrival. The others rose, going to their separate rooms to gather their belongings, such as they were. Pyle's wife quickly, dutifully, collected the dishes from the table.

Tom Quinn guided Jody Short to the front room and sat him down where Mike Hancock could keep an eye on the kid, and then wandered out on to the front porch of the stage station to study the paling desert sky. He braced his hands on the hitch rail, asking himself what sort of fool he was.

The hostler, a bad-tempered, narrow, dark-eyed man was leading the hitched team and stagecoach round. A different set of horses, of course, and Tom Quinn stepped from the plankwalk to make their acquaintance. The vastly experienced Tank Dawson had told him it was useful to introduce himself to the animals. Each team, he had explained, was different, each with its own foibles, like humans. Quinn didn't totally understand what Tank had been talking about, but in a way it seemed to make sense, and so he paused at each horse's head, stroking its muzzle and speaking softly to it.

Then Quinn started back toward the station to tell those waiting that the stage was ready. Apparently the hostler had already made that announcement, for before Quinn could enter the building George Sabato slipped through the door carrying the heavy canvas sack he had been guarding. His eyes flickered nervously up and down the street; his pudgy hand did not stray far from the skirt of his coat, which concealed a sidearm.

'Need help, Sabato?' Quinn asked with a slight smile.

'I'll tell you if I do,' Sabato snapped back. His nerves were obviously on edge. His reputation and livelihood, Quinn guessed, hung on safely delivering the gold to the prison authorities in Yuma.

The door remained open and after a minute or two the other passengers emerged: Lily Davenport carrying a small carpetbag with her overnight things in it, Jody Short with Mike Hancock directly behind him, looking gray-faced and drawn this morning. Probably what Mike needed more than anything just now was sleep, a scarce commodity when your task is to watch a killer twenty-four hours a day.

'You all right, Mike?' Quinn asked as, together, they half-aided, half-forced Jody Short up into the stage where he sat opposite Lily.

'I'm all right,' Mike replied with a weariness that did little to convince Quinn. 'I guess I'd better sit up on the box with you. If there's more trouble ahead. . . .' His voice trailed off. His eyes pleaded that there would be no more trouble on the last leg into Yuma.

'It'd probably be best,' Quinn agreed. 'If you don't mind eating some dust.'

'As if the dust don't blow inside these coaches!' Mike said, offering a weak smile.

That was true enough. The side curtains on the coach did little but darken the interior. Just now the four curtains were rolled up as the morning remained cool. Hancock took a moment to hold George Sabato aside and Quinn heard him say in a low voice, 'Make sure you keep that pistol of yours far away from the kid.'

'Do I look like an idiot?' Sabato asked angrily. 'Remember, I was a prison guard for a long while.'

Mike Hancock nodded an apology and clambered up into the box to seat himself beside Quinn who had gathered the reins by now. The marshal muttered, 'He don't look like an idiot, but he sure talks like one.'

Quinn laughed out loud, turned to wave farewell to Aaron Pyle and his wife, standing in the doorway of the stage station, and cracked the whip above the lead horses' ears.

With the new sun low and red at their backs, the team lurched into motion and the stagecoach rolled forward out of the pueblo of Las Palmas, carrying its diverse and unpredictable cargo on toward Yuma across the white sand desert.

The morning was still cool, the team fresh and eager to run, and Quinn's mood lightened as he now foresaw a quick and easy run into the town. Mike Hancock beside him rode silently, clutching his rifle. From time to time the marshal's eyelids dropped and Quinn had to elbow Mike to keep him awake. Not only did he need an alert guard, but asleep, Hancock could easily be jounced from the seat to fall against the sand or be rolled over by the coach's wheels. 'Sorry,' the marshal murmured more than once.

A quarter of a mile on the man standing in the middle of the road with a shotgun in his hands halted the stagecoach.

Quinn's first impulse was to run the man down, but then he saw the surrey drawn to the side of the road, saw a Spanish-dressed woman in black standing near it, leather satchel clutched in her small hands, and though he told Mike Hancock to stay wary, Quinn did not take it for a hold-up attempt.

The man, thick shouldered, rough-appearing, wearing a thick bandito-style mustache approached the stage and shouted up to Quinn.

'My daughter, she needs to go to Yuma. We had trouble with a wheel on the road. I could not make the station before you left. I will pay whatever you want now, but she must go to Yuma.' Quinn glanced at the small Spanish girl who had turned her eyes down shyly, then looked back to the grim face of her father who still held his shotgun tightly. 'It's all right with me,' he answered. 'You ride on into Las Palmas and pay the station master there after we've gone.'

'I will do that, I promise, *señor*.' There was relief

and sincerity in the big man's eyes. Personally Quinn could not care less whether or not he took an extra passenger on to Yuma, but he knew the Spanish man would feel he had not met his obligation if he did not pay for his daughter's passage.

Therefore, with Mike Hancock holding the reins, Quinn stowed the young woman's small bag in the boot and helped her aboard the stage where three sets of appraising eyes studied her closely. Sabato just seemed puzzled, Jody Short wolfishly interested; Lily Davenport's gaze was one of inspection and assessment.

Climbing back up on to the box, Quinn took the reins from Mike, situated them in his gloved fingers and started the team westward once again.

'That was kind of funny, wasn't it?' the marshal asked after another mile or so.

'What?'

'I mean, stopping the stage like that. He said he'd had trouble with a wheel, but if so, how did he manage to fix it again way out here?'

'I guess he's handy,' Quinn said with a smile.

'I've been a lawman too long, Quinn,' Mike Hancock answered. 'It makes a man suspicious of everything and everyone, I guess. But I was wondering if . . . maybe the man didn't go into Las Palmas because he didn't want his face to be seen.'

Quinn guided the team onward across the barren flats. His answer was vague if not unconcerned. 'It's a mysterious life, Mike.'

'Isn't it,' the marshal agreed and he leaned back, tilting his hat forward against the glare the white-sand desert reflected from the rising sun.

The horses ran on easily. The land rolled past – a land remarkable for the absence of landmarks of any kind. Endless sand, scattered creosote and clumps of nopal cactus, little else. Quinn fell into silent concentration. He considered Mike Hancock's words only once and then dismissed the assumption. What did it matter to them anyway if the big Spaniard was a wanted man?

Still, it was a little puzzling if one thought about it. But then, as he had said to Hancock, it's a mysterious world we live in, never knowing the comings and goings, the intent of those around us. We can only accept what we are told. Wild surmise can lead to dangerous conclusions.

Yet . . . the young Spanish girl did seem to be a mysterious presence among them and they needed no more problems than they already had riding with them.

The stage rolled on farther across the white wilderness carrying more questions than answers.

FOUR

Her name was Alicia. Quinn found that much out as they halted the team at the Tortuga Creek crossing around noon to let the horses water and rest. There was scrub willow along the brightly flowing creek and a thicket of mesquite trees along the sandy shore where the passengers gathered what relief they could from the sun in the lacy shade the thorny plants offered. The girl had been standing apart from the rest of them, hands clasped together in front of her. Her dark eyes were wide and slightly timorous when she lifted them at Quinn's approach.

Quinn stretched the truth when he told her, 'I need your name to write down in my register. The company likes to keep records, you see?'

She only continued to stare up at him like a small animal trying to decide whether to bolt or not. Tom Quinn wondered whether perhaps the girl did not speak English. He began trying to frame his question in Spanish for her, but she suddenly blurted out:

'Alicia,' and spun away to walk off through the vague dry shade of the thicket.

That was all the information Quinn got from her. Well, the girl had her secrets – they all did on this run, it seemed. There was no point in pressing inquiries further. Quinn had no register, had no reason beyond curiosity to even be asking the girl that much. Shrugging, he returned to the creek where the horses, up to their hocks in the stream, drank. Mike Hancock held the reins to the team. Quinn dipped his hat into the creek and emptied it on his head.

'Learn anything?' the marshal asked.

'Her name is Alicia,' Quinn answered. Then he took the reins from Mike and backed the team on to dry land so that the passengers could climb aboard the coach again. The two saddle horses which had been untethered to drink were again tied on behind the stage.

They continued then, following the old stage

road up out of the river bottom on to the white flats once again. The sun assaulted them. The hot winds gusted intermittently. The horses, no longer so fresh, had to be urged on to speed now and then. Inside the coach the passengers bounced and careered into one another as the hot dust crept in around the margins of the curtains. Mike Hancock spotted them fast, and he lifted a gloved hand toward the mounted men sitting their horses motionlessly on the road ahead. 'I don't think these men are waiting for a ride,' the marshal muttered, levering a round into the receiver of his Winchester. Tom Quinn slowed the team. What was there to do? These were men who meant them no good. Five of them, Quinn counted. It would do no good to try to run through them. They would catch the coach quickly. There was nowhere to veer from the coach road. Their wheels would swiftly sink into the white sands.

'It must be the gold they're after,' Hancock guessed.

'It seems likely,' Quinn said grimly as he slowed the team still more. 'If that's all they want, I say let them have it.'

'You are not a lawman,' Mike Hancock answered

with determination. 'I can't just sit here and watch a hold-up.'

'Mike,' Quinn cautioned. 'You aren't going to fight off five men. As you can see, I've got my hands full. Besides, starting a fight might mean that one of the passengers will catch a stray bullet. We've got to let them have the gold if that's what they want.'

Mike Hancock frowned, ground his teeth together and tightened his grip on his rifle as Quinn halted his shuddering team. The waiting men circled the coach, guns in hand. They did not wear masks. That indicated not carelessness to Tom Quinn, but a lack of concern about being identified.

Mike Hancock recognized their leader as he neared the stage. The marshal hissed: 'Guerrero!'

It was indeed Ernesto Guerrero. Quinn glanced at the narrow dark face with its neatly trimmed mustache, the black expressionless eyes. The rumor that he was still imprisoned down in Riodoso was obviously wrong.

Guerrero walked his horse nearer, his Colt held loosely in his right hand. Two rough-looking men flanked him. One a thick dark Mexican, the other a pale blond kid whose eyes held a vaguely

54

unsettled look.

The movement that Guerrero made was sudden and unexpected. Quinn was never sure if the border raider had recognized Hancock or only seen the badge on his shirt front. Nor was he sure that Mike had not fired first with his Winchester. Two shots rang out almost in unison. Mike half-rose from the bench of the coach, looked skyward and toppled to the earth below. The horses reared and strained at the reins and Quinn had to settle the team. There was no chance for him to draw his gun even had he been inclined to follow Hancock's folly of facing down five armed men.

'You,' Guerrero said to Quinn, not yet holstering his smoking pistol. 'Hold the team steady and do not try for a weapon.' The bandit did not recognize Tom Quinn as one of the posse that had chased him from the Yavapai range. On that occasion they had never gotten close enough to Guerrero himself for the outlaw to have seen Quinn.

'I'm holding them,' Quinn said in a flat voice. His boot was braced against the wooden brake handle, his gloved hands tight around the reins. He looked to where Mike Hancock lay unmoving against the hot sand, his rifle beside him, and his mouth tightened. So Mike had made his last run as well. If the marshal had maintained his patience just a little while longer he might have ended up, as he wished, running a stage station, or as a settled bank guard somewhere. Mike Hancock, Quinn decided, had had too much of a sense of duty for his own good.

'Toss down your weapon,' Quinn was advised. He slicked his Colt from his holster, reversed it, and tossed it to the bandit sitting his horse nearest him. Glancing to his left, Quinn did see a bright object on the seat beside him. It was Mike Hancock's pistol, fallen from his holster in the brief struggle. The bandits had not searched Hancock's body. What threat was the marshal to them now, armed or unarmed?

With infinite caution, his eyes on the outlaws even as he seemed to be studying the distances, Quinn scooted Hancock's .44 along the seat and managed to slip the pistol behind his belt, under his loose shirt. The weapon would do him no good just now, but it was a comfort having it.

No one had been alerted by his furtive movements. The bandits' eyes were fixed on something else, and now Quinn saw what it was.

Lily Davenport had leaped down from the stage.

Ernesto Guerrero had dismounted and she rushed into his arms, kissing his throat and lips. 'I knew you'd come,' she said, 'but I didn't count on seeing you 'til Yuma!'

'This is much safer,' Quinn heard Guerrero say. With the girl in his arms he ordered his men, 'Rafael, Lon, search the other passengers for weapons.'

The two who had been flanking Guerrero, his chief lieutenants it seemed – the bulky Mexican, Rafael and the narrow American, Lon – swung down from their saddles and opened both stagecoach doors. In a minute they emerged, Lon holding up the pistol which Quinn recognized as George Sabato's Remington .36 revolver.

'This is all,' the blond kid said. 'Say, Guerrero, there's a man in there wearing shackles.'

'Is there?' the bandit leader said with little apparent interest. He was still distracted, fascinated by the woman in his arms.

'That's not all,' Rafael said. The bulky Mexican was grinning widely, showing gold teeth. 'There is also a pretty little girl here.'

The other bandits drew nearer, their interest piqued. From horseback, one of them lifted the side curtain to peer in at Alicia. 'I would like a piece of that,' Quinn heard one of the border raiders say.

'I saw her first,' Rafael said with just a hint of menace.

'Leave her alone,' Ernesto Guerrero told them. 'There are plenty of women back at Soledad.'

To Quinn it seemed that the outlaw was not speaking out of any concern for Alicia, but only to head off a fight among his men before it could get started. Nevertheless he was glad for Guerrero's intervention.

Because otherwise, he, like Mike Hancock, might just have thrown caution to the winds and drawn the hidden Colt to shoot down any man who tried to get rough with Alicia.

Guerrero now stepped back from the coach and looked to the surrounding desert, assuring himself that there was no sign of immediate danger. He still held Lily Davenport's hand – where had these two met? – but now he dropped it as he explained to the woman:

'I did not bring a buggy for you – we couldn't be sure that you were on the stage. If you will get back aboard, we will travel the rest of the way to Soledad. By evening, you shall have the comfort of a warm bath and a silken bed.' Lily wore an expression of dazed gratitude. However Guerrero had charmed her, he had done his work well.

'You, driver!' the bandit leader called up. 'What's your name?'

'Quinn,' Tom answered. Guerrero shrugged as if the name meant nothing to him. There was no reason why it should.

'Quinn, you are to ride inside the coach as well. My man, Paco here, can handle a team and he knows the way.'

'Why should I go along?' Quinn asked as a spiderlike, younger outlaw clambered up toward the driver's box.

'Would you prefer, Quinn, to be left alone out on this desert? You would have no hope of reaching Yuma, you realize.'

Quinn did realize it. The miles of white sand, the blistering heat of the sun would defeat him before he could walk even a few miles. He handed the leather ribbons over to Paco, swung down and stepped back into the stagecoach where he had begun this unfortunate journey.

With a crack of the whip the stage lurched into motion once again, driven by the spidery Paco whose idea of driving seemed to be to yell as frequently as possible and to continually pop the long whip above the ears of the team. The stagecoach was flanked by Guerrero's riders, although Quinn did not see Ernesto himself as they rolled southward along a barely visible track across the white sand.

George Sabato had a worried look on his red face. He tried to catch Quinn's eyes as if to plead for help, but Tom just shook his head slightly. Guerrero seemed to know nothing about the gold. He hadn't asked about it or even looked through the boot. Apparently his mission had been accomplished: he had gotten Lily Davenport. With luck, the bandits would not even bother to look under the luggage in the boot and discover the heavy canvas sack. Lily knew nothing about the gold, nor did Jody Short. Perhaps, having reached Soledad, Guerrero would simply release them to continue their trip to Yuma. After all, what use did the outlaw have for any of them?

It was, Quinn decided, a scant hope, but then our lives hinge on such concepts. Truly, none of them except Lily Davenport could guess what the future held for them.

Jody Short tried yet another ploy in his search for freedom.

'Ma'am? Lily? When we get to where we're going,

do you think Guerrero can have these shackles struck from me?'

'I have no idea what Ernesto will do,' the lady said in the chilly tone of voice she had used when she thought that Quinn was refusing her wishes.

'But you could talk to him, couldn't you?' Short asked, leaning forward, his eyes as earnest as he could make them.

'I advise Ernesto on nothing. He does what he wishes.'

'But if he was to ask you . . .' Jody went on, a little more panic-stricken. 'I mean, we've talked quite a bit, you and I. I'd be happy to join up with Guerrero if he wanted me.'

'Why would you?' Lily asked, her eyes half-closed now against the dust blowing into the coach.

'I don't understand,' Jody answered, perplexed.

'You are an innocent man, you told me,' Lily said. 'Why then would you now be willing to take up the outlaw trail?' Lily leaned back now and closed her eyes all the way. 'You can't have it both ways, Jody Short. Either you are a killer and would be willing to ride with Ernesto's gang, or you are innocent of killing that young woman and have no business among the outlaws.'

Jody cast about in his mind for a reply, but did not find one. He leaned back with a small moan and closed his own eyes.

Quinn had listened to the conversation, but his eyes had been fixed on Alicia the entire time. Her dark eyes sparked and then grew cold. Her hands were clenched into fists so tightly that her knuckles had turned white. She was rigid in her seat as if she would hurl herself forward.

Quinn could only shake his head. There was too much going on for a simple man like him. He only wanted to shake loose from this situation and somehow make his way back to his ranch in the hills along the Yavapai where tall pines grew in long ranks and the breeze from the mountains cooled the long land.

In another hour, with Paco berating the horses and cracking the long whip all the way, they began to slow. Glancing out, Quinn saw scattered adobe houses, low and sun-baked, here and there a few desert-stunted willows, indicating some source of water nearby, and then with a following whirlwind of dust, the horses were reined in roughly, the brake applied and they found themselves in the heart of the outlaw town, Soledad.

The dust settled slowly. Quinn saw more adobe

brick buildings, these clustered together, nearly shoulder to shoulder, lining what might have been described as a street. Now Guerrero did reappear; apparently he had been riding behind the coach to watch for any possible pursuit. He was trail-dusty and the clothes he wore were dirty, but he smiled broadly, revealing a perfect set of white teeth. Lily Davenport, leaning halfway out the window of the coach, nearly gurgled with delight at this handsome figure of a man. A rustler, a killer, an outlaw – as she must have known. But who knew what secret dreams lurk in a woman's heart? Maybe she was simply blind to Guerrero's widely-known viciousness, took all of the tales about him to be lies.

No matter, the lady was in love. That much was obvious.

Lily leaped from the stage without waiting for anyone to assist her, and Guerrero swung down from his tall paint pony. They embraced again and Guerrero whispered something into Lily's ear which made her laugh, blush, and laugh again.

With his arm around Lily's waist, Guerrero shouted out commands in Spanish to his men, then turned Lily toward the open door of a low building where two people, a man and a woman, stood awaiting his approach, smiles creasing their dark faces. Guerrero and Lily entered the building, the plank door was closed, and the rest of the passengers waited in the stifling heat to consider their fates.

'Listen to me,' Quinn whispered, leaning forward so that his forehead nearly touched Alicia's, 'you are my wife, got that?'

Alicia's dark eyes widened but she only nodded. She whispered urgently, 'That woman, Lily, she will know I am not.'

'No, she won't. You and I had a fight. You didn't want to come back to me. Your father made you, so he stopped the stage to make sure that we were together again.'

Alicia was thoughtful. She shook her head negatively. 'The other woman will not believe this.'

'For the time being she has other things on her mind,' Quinn said. 'It's not safe for you to be alone with these men, understand?'

Again she nodded. There was no fear in her eyes, only doubt. Neither Jody Short nor George Sabato, struggling with their own concerns, seemed to have heard a word of the whispered conversation.

In another minute, Lon approached the coach.

Apparently he had been put in charge of the prisoners because he was an American. Most of the other bandits seemed to speak no or only a smattering of English. Lon was hardly alone. Behind him in a shadow cast by the pueblo, there were three armed bandits watching them with wary, dark eyes.

Lon tried a smile, but it was evident that the pale-eyed outlaw had little experience of using that expression. His eyes swept across Alicia and then fixed on those of Tom Quinn, hardening as they did. Lon had already measured his men and he knew which among them was the dangerous one.

'Welcome to Pueblo Soledad, folks. Step down and I'll show you to your accommodations.'

FIVE

The four of them – Quinn, Alicia, George Sabato, and Jody Short still in shackles – were herded into the low-roofed adobe with rough bunks positioned along the walls. Despite the lack of furnishings and no visible help, Quinn wondered if the building hadn't been intended to serve as some sort of crude hotel when it was constructed. Otherwise, it seemed to serve no discernible purpose.

Sabato paced the floor after their guards had gone outside and closed the heavy plank door behind them. Jody Short sank on to one of the cots and complained bitterly, 'If I don't get these manacles off, they're going to have to amputate my hands. Look at my wrists!' He held them up, but collected no sympathy.

Quinn sat on a bed along the opposite wall and pulled Alicia down to sit beside him. He doubted that anyone believed his hastily concocted tale about Alicia being his changeable wife, but it seemed prudent to carry on with the charade. Alicia sat staring at the floor, hands between her skirted legs for a long minute. Then she shifted her gaze to Quinn's face and asked in an urgent whisper:

'What can we do now?'

'Very little,' Quinn had to tell her. 'We'll just have to wait until we have a chance – or until Guerrero decides our fate.'

'I don't think he will kill us,' Alicia said with groundless optimism.

'Maybe not, but I don't think he'll want us going on to Yuma to tell the law where he's hiding out.'

Sabato had heard a part of that. Now he stopped his pacing long enough to ask: 'Say, which side of the border are we on? Is this Mexico or isn't it?'

'I can't see that it matters,' Quinn answered. 'Not to us.'

'I suppose not,' Sabato grumbled. He resumed his pacing, still obviously concerned about the gold and what failing to deliver it to Yuma would mean to his career.

'I'll try to make sure you get through to Yuma,' Quinn told Alicia. 'Somehow.'

'It doesn't matter,' she said bitterly. 'I don't care about Yuma.'

Quinn frowned. The girl had been so adamant about reaching Yuma. She and her father had stopped the stage *en route*. Now she no longer cared? Perhaps she had been running on some sort of timetable which could not now be met. He sighed.

Maybe she was just as changeable as their transparent tale indicated.

'Get some sleep,' Quinn said, patting the bunk. 'I'll move over to that empty one.'

'Won't that look suspicious?' Alicia asked, and her black eyes twinkled slightly with faint amusement.

'I think that anyone would understand that these are not normal circumstances,' Tom said, smiling for the first time in a long while.

Alicia nodded and began removing the comb from her hair. Tom Quinn rose and she tilted her head back. 'Shouldn't you at least kiss me goodnight?' she asked.

'I suppose that would look better,' he said. He leaned toward her, received a kiss as light as a butterfly's touch and walked away, wondering. As he seated himself on the next bunk along the wall he glanced back at her. Her raven-black hair now fell free across her shoulders. Her hint of a smile was gone. Alicia now sat on the cot staring across the room with ill-concealed venom.

Tom shook his head slightly. The woman was a mystery, and it seemed that was the way she wanted it. He gave up on trying to figure out matters for this night. He was bone-tired, he had developed a dull headache. Without removing his boots he stretched out on the cot, watching with one eye open until Sabato, finished with his useless pacing, lay on one of the opposite bunks and pulled a blanket across him. Jody Short also stretched out.

They tried to sleep then, with varying degrees of success as the smoky lantern burned low and cast wavering shadows across the walls. Quinn had little reason for optimism, but he was not completely disheartened. After all, Guerrero had not immediately killed them all – maybe that was Lily's influence, who could tell? They were still alive and so there was still hope.

The other reason for Quinn's distant optimism was the cool weight of the .44 Colt nestled against his spine.

They would play hell trying to get that from him.

There was a dull red dawn light glowing in the high window of the 'hotel' when the door burst open and two men – Rafael and another bandit Quinn had not seen before – stamped into the room. *This is it*, Quinn thought, sitting up sharply. His hand caressed the butt of the pistol behind his belt, and he braced himself. But the reason for their visit was one he could not have expected or foreseen. The men ignored him, ignored Alicia, paid no attention to the sleep-fuddled George Sabato. They walked directly to Jody Short's bunk and roused him.

'Come on,' Rafael said in heavily accented English, 'we're taking you to get those irons off.'

Jody rose to his feet swiftly. Quinn heard him say exultantly, 'I knew Lily would come through for me.'

Had she? Hadn't she? Quinn had no way of knowing. He rose, stretched and went to sit beside Alicia who was trying to pin her hair up again.

'I need a mirror,' she complained. 'There's one in my bag.'

The bandits had not allowed them to remove their belongings from the stagecoach. Perhaps that was a good sign. Perhaps that meant they would be allowed to travel on soon. Perhaps it meant nothing at all. Quinn was growing tired of the confusion. The waiting.

'I don't think they even looked in the boot,' Sabato said from across the room on hearing Alicia's complaint. And that brought a weak smile to the stout little man's lips. He was still hoping that somehow the hidden gold would not be discovered. Maybe it wouldn't; maybe they would be allowed to continue their journey – that all depended on Guerrero's mood. Which, Quinn reflected, should be lighter on this particular morning. They needed to talk to him.

'Your hair looks fine,' Quinn told Alicia, brushing back a dark tendril from her forehead.

'It does not!' she snapped back.

She swept his hand away and rose to her feet to stand glowering into the shadowed interior of the low adobe. Quinn hesitated and then rose to stand beside her.

'I'm sorry,' he said. 'I didn't mean to make you angry.'

'It's not you,' she said, when her angered breathing had slowed.

'What, then?'

Alicia turned to face him, her cheeks paling as her flush retreated. Her hand trembled as she reached for him, changed her mind and folded them together. She bowed her head.

'Him,' she said in a throttled voice. 'They're going to turn him loose.'

'Jody Short?'

'Yes, him!' Her head lifted and her eyes met his again. 'He is supposed to die and they are going to release him.'

'Maybe. What if they do?' Quinn asked, his frown deepening.

'You know my name?' she asked. He hesitated, looking for an answer. With a small shrug he responded:

'Alicia.'

'Yes. My name is Alicia . . . *Delgado.*'

`The murdered girl . . . Quinn said uncertainly.

'Yes. She was my sister.' Her eyes searched his anxiously, intently. When she spoke it was with extreme bitterness. 'I was going to Yuma to make sure he was hung. I did not know he was on that stagecoach.'

'But they would have notified you,' Quinn said.

'I understand that there are certain legal things . . . appeals, that can be filed and delay the execution, even suspend the sentence.'

'That's true,' Quinn admitted, 'but—'

'And in this case there was no witness to the crime, or so they say. They might wonder if Jody Short had really done it, or if the jury was mistaken. They might have let him off.'

'It's possible, if unlikely,' Quinn said.

'That cannot be allowed to happen. Quinn – I was there that day. I saw him murder my sister.'

'But, then. . . ?'

'That was what I was going to tell them in Yuma if he was not hung without my testimony. My father did not want me to go, but I am a determined woman.'

'So it would seem. Sit down and tell me about it,' Quinn suggested. Alicia was still trembling with anger. She seemed to wobble on her feet. He took her elbow and sat her on the bunk again. Across the room Sabato, remarkably, had fallen back to sleep.

'My sister and I were riding early in the morning. My horse caught a stone in its hoof and I told Dolores to ride ahead, I would catch up. I heard strange sounds, a muted cry, and I crept forward, leading my horse. And I saw them . . . him atop her.' For a moment Alicia's grief overwhelmed her fury. She calmed herself and went on.

'I saw him kill Dolores. What could I do? I had no gun. I ran away! Coward that I am.'

'You would have just gotten yourself hurt,' Quinn said.

'Perhaps. I rode then, rode back to my father's rancho. He swore he would get Short, but by the time he had gathered his mounted vaqueros from the line camps, word came that the sheriff had already captured Short. My father begged me to not get involved in the trial. He said that if the man was released, my life would be in danger as well. And so I remained silent. He was right, it seems. Jody Short was convicted anyway. But now he is free again!' she said in an agonized voice.

'Maybe, for the time being,' Quinn replied. The anguished young woman moved to him, leaned her head against his chest and slipped her arms around him. It took Quinn a moment to figure what the girl had in mind.

She slipped the gun from behind his belt and turned to rush away. Quinn was just able to catch her arm and turn her back, wrenching the Colt from her hand.

'Let me do it! I want to kill him!' Alicia spat as

she writhed in his arms. Her voice was loud enough to rouse Sabato from his sleep.

'Not here. Not now,' Quinn said positively. 'There are a dozen armed men out there. How far do you think they'd let you get? Besides,' he added, 'this pistol may be our only chance to save our own lives.'

'What's happening?' Sabato asked. He sat up on his bunk, rubbing the back of his thick neck.

'Nothing,' Quinn answered, 'the girl's upset.'

Sabato nodded, asking no more questions. The simple concept of a hysterical female was an explanation he could understand.

'Where's Guerrero, anyway?' Sabato said as he rose to tuck in his shirt and stamp into his boots. His voice was absurdly officious, as if he were going to take Guerrero to task.

'I couldn't guess,' Quinn answered woodenly. Sitting beside him on the bunk now, Alicia continued to be flooded with the sort of fury that would do her no good at all. Her fingernails dug into his arm and now and then a tight hiss escaped from between her teeth He had no doubt that she would have shot Jody Short had she gotten the opportunity. He tried to keep her calm, because, important as her hatred of Short was to her, it might also impede any chance of his own objective succeeding. She wanted Short dead; he was determined to find a way to get Alicia and himself out of Soledad alive.

An hour later a message from Guerrero arrived.

It was the fat man, Rafael who entered the room, although they could clearly see two other men waiting outside in the bright sunlight. Rafael approached them and said in good, if halting English:

'Guerrero wants to see you now.'

'And about time, too,' George Sabato said, reaching for his hat.

'Not you!' Rafael said sharply. 'The man Quinn and his wife.'

Quinn nodded, rose and whispered to Alicia: 'Remember our story.' She nodded and Rafael, stony-faced, let them precede him to the door. Quinn wondered whether the Mexican would be able to make out the form of the pistol butt beneath his loose shirt, but apparently he was not that sharp-eyed. Nothing was said as they stepped out into the heat of the day and were marched to the open door of the building next door, the one they had seen Guerrero and Lily Davenport disappear into the day before.

The interior of the adobe building was cool. It boasted a wooden floor which was waxed and unscarred. There was a native stone fireplace with an old Kentucky rifle on hooks above it and striped Navajo rugs were scattered about. A brown leather sofa and matching chair completed the furnishings.

As Quinn and Alicia were shown in Lily Davenport, wearing a flouncy white dress which certainly had not come across country with her, walked forward to greet them. Her manner was that of lady of the manor as she seated them on the leather sofa. Her eyes sparkled nearly as brightly as the diamond necklace she wore. No one knew what to say, so they sat in silence for another minute before Ernesto Guerrero, in dark trousers, a gleaming white shirt and bolo tie appeared. The bandit leader was smiling. Quinn could not decide whether the expression eased his doubts or made him more uncomfortable. As Guerrero sat in the leather chair, Lily seated herself on its overstuffed arm and they all considered one another. Guerrero spoke first.

'Quinn, Lily has told me what you did for her along the trail. If not for you, she says the Apaches would probably have captured her. Or worse.'

Quinn only nodded, not knowing where this was leading. Guerrero continued:

'Mrs Quinn,' the outlaw said to Alicia whose response to that form of address was a blank stare. There was an amused glow in Lily's eyes. Alicia had been right – the woman was not fooled, but she let Guerrero go on, resting her ringed hand on his shoulder.

'Mrs Quinn, I know who you are,' Guerrero said, leaning back more deeply into the chair.

'Do you?' Alicia said without expression.

'Yes, I think so. Lily has told me the circumstances of your boarding the stagecoach. She also was able to give me a description of the man who put you aboard it. Your father.' Still Alicia did not respond and so Guerrero continued:

'Unless I miss my guess, your name is Delgado. Your father, Vicente Delgado and I once did some business together. Not so long ago I was invited to his rancho, and I saw you briefly. Am I wrong?'

'No.'

'I did not think so.' Guerrero rose to his feet. 'I know your father. Well. I know that if he finds that you are missing, he will comb this desert until he finds you. And I know this – Vicente is a proud and vengeful man if he thinks he has been insulted.'

'Where is this leading?' Quinn wanted to know. Guerrero smiled crookedly.

'I cannot insult Vicente Delgado. You, Quinn, saved Lily's life. You do not work for the stage line, do you?'

'No, it was only a matter of necessity, my driving that coach.'

'So I have been given to understand.' Guerrero paused, stroking his chin. 'You have no reason to care whether the stage reaches Yuma or not?'

'No.'

'Where would you go. . . ?' Guerrero glanced at Lily and then returned his dark eyes to Quinn and Alicia. 'Where would you go if I let you have the two saddle horses you brought with you?'

Quinn answered, 'Back to Vicente Delgado's rancho, of course. First to show her father that Alicia was safe, and then – I think we would try again to settle down there. If Alicia will still have me.'

'I wish you luck there, Quinn. She is a fine-looking young woman. I suppose it may seem that I have not come directly to the point. Quinn, I owe you a debt for saving Lily. Mrs Quinn, I will not offend your father. I cannot, however, risk having you two ride to Yuma to report what has happened.

If you are determined to return to Vicente Delgado's rancho, and give me your word that you will remain silent, all I can say is that I will have your horses saddled, and *vaya con Dios.*'

Quinn said nothing for a minute, but he could feel relief loosening his cramped muscles. Things could hardly have gone any better.

'Have you any clothes to ride in?' he asked Alicia.

'In my bag. Tell me, Guerrero,' she went on without apparent unease, 'what about the young man? The one who wore shackles? What will you do with him?'

Guerrero shrugged indifferently. 'I can always use more men. I have taken him on in . . . what do you say? A probationary status.'

Alicia's eyes had gone cold again, that terrible coal-black glare had returned. Quinn spoke up to distract her.

'And the other passenger? The fat man?'

'About him, I have not yet decided. But do not concern yourself with it, Quinn. I promise you that I am not a cruel man.' Which might have convinced Quinn had he not seen some of the work Guerrero and his raiders had done up along the Yavapai Range. Perhaps the man was only

80

trying to convince Lily that the popular conception of him was wrong. Who knew? It didn't matter at the moment. They had been granted a reprieve, although Quinn believed it was more a matter of Guerrero fearing a reprisal from Vicente Delgado than out of gratitude to Quinn for having saved Lily.

No matter – they had been set free by the outlaw leader, and this was not the time to debate the reasons behind it, but only to take full advantage. And immediately, before Guerrero could change his mind.

'Where do we find the horses?' Quinn asked rising. He had to reach behind him to grab Alicia's hand and tug her to her feet. He was frightened of what the impulsive girl might say next.

'Do you know Rafael? He will show you where they are,' Guerrero answered. He followed them partway to the open door and waited until Quinn was three steps from the threshold before adding in a low, ominous voice that Lily Davenport could not have heard.

'Do not disappoint me, Quinn.'

SIX

'Just keep moving,' Quinn hissed into Alicia's ear as he guided her by the elbow to where Rafael and two other bandits stood in the shade of the awning, studying them. Glancing behind them once, Quinn saw Guerrero flick a hand in a small gesture of command. Tom Quinn was not so sure even now that they were going to be set free. The signal to his men could have meant anything.

Alicia seemed determined to speak her mind, to return to the adobe. This was not the time for that. It was time to try to make their break from the outlaw camp. Quinn had already decided that if there was treachery afoot, he would snake his Colt from behind his belt and go to shooting if that seemed to be the only way out.

He would set Alicia free one way or the other.

The outlaws' suspicious eyes remained fixed on them, their weapons at the ready, as Quinn and Alicia swung aboard the saddle ponies. Quinn was riding Mike Hancock's gray, Alicia Jody Short's buckskin. Alicia now wore black jeans and a white throat-high blouse, retrieved from the boot of the stagecoach. She had been forced to change in the stable behind one of the stall partitions, but she had not complained. She left her dress and traveling bag behind them. Perhaps now she was beginning to feel the urgency that Tom Quinn felt. Who knew what the outlaws were thinking? Who knew when Guerrero, given time to reconsider, might change his mind about letting them go free?

Quinn could almost feel the eyes of the bandits on his back as they trailed out of town toward the east, but no shots were fired, no voices raised. Within thirty minutes they were out on to the open desert. Tom Quinn swiveled frequently in his saddle to watch the backtrail, but he saw no sign of pursuing horsemen.

It was past midday, the sun still riding high. They pressed on across the white sand until they reached a low knoll studded with nopal cactus and yucca. There Quinn called a halt and swung down from the gray horse's back to let their mounts rest. There was no shade, so he and Alicia sat side by side on a sun-heated flat stone, sipping water from their canteen. In a few hours it would be cool; Tom planned on riding through the evening as long as possible. At some point he meant to intersect the stage road again, send Alicia on her way and turn his own horse homeward, toward the Yavapai country.

They had been extremely lucky, he considered as he watched Alicia tilt back her head and allow the canteen water to trickle down her throat. Anything might have happened back there. As the dry wind drifted a few loose strands of dark hair across Alicia's forehead and a small swarm of gnats raised from somewhere to harry them, the woman finally corked the canteen, handed it back to Quinn and smiled.

'Well, then, we have fooled them,' she said.

'I don't know about that.' Quinn continued to stare out across the long desert flats. 'You were right, Lily never believed our story.'

'That's not what I mean,' Alicia said, her eyes meeting him with a subdued urgency. 'They think we have ridden away to my father's rancho.'

Quinn frowned. 'What do you mean? That is

84

exactly what we are doing.'

'No!' Alicia said, rising to her feet to stand, hands on hips, studying the raw land stretched out before them. 'That is what I wanted them to think.' She crouched down, put her hand on Quinn's wrist and said with all sincerity:

'We must sneak back into Soledad and kill Jody Short.'

'You can't be serious,' Quinn said, laughing explosively.

'Of course I am,' Alicia said, looking at Quinn as if he had just fallen a notch or two in her estimation. 'If he can escape the law, he cannot escape me. He murdered my sister, don't forget.'

'I haven't forgotten, but what you are proposing is madness, Alicia.'

'You won't go with me?' she asked, her hand falling away from his wrist.

'No.'

'Then you must give me the pistol,' she said defiantly. Quinn laughed again, but there was little humor in it.

'I don't think so. I've been trying to keep you alive, not send you off to get killed.'

'I think you do not understand honor. A debt of blood.' She was now petulant and pleading at once.

'I think maybe I do, but I don't understand suicide. There's no way anything can be done in Soledad. You saw how things are. Guerrero has at least a dozen men there. Maybe more. What do you think you could do against them?'

'I don't know! I don't care! So long as I kill Jody Short before they capture me. Will you give me the pistol?'

'No.'

'I think maybe you are a coward,' she said accusingly.

'I think maybe I am not a madman,' Quinn heard himself saying. She had turned her slender back to him, her arms crossed beneath her breasts. 'Alicia – tell me this – if you knew that Jody Short was on that stage, why didn't your father raid it and take him away?'

'We did not know,' Alicia said, turning slightly toward him. Her words were brittle, dry as the desert heat. 'Even if we had, Father could not risk a gamble like that. It would draw too much attention to him.'

'Attention?'

Alicia flipped a hand in a vague gesture. 'He has been trying to keep himself veiled from the law. There was . . . some trouble on the rancho recently.'

86

'What do you mean?' Quinn asked, rising from the flat rock now. He turned Alicia and looked down into her dark eyes. 'What exactly did happen down there? What does your father do? Tell me.'

'Oh it's nothing to tell,' Alicia said lightly. Then she began shuddering and Quinn wrapped his arms around her, holding her tightly to him until she said explosively: 'I hate it!' and pushed away from him.

Quinn released her. Apparently what Guerrero had intimated was true. He and Vicente Delgado were sometime associates, both involved with the border raiders. It seemed they did not like each other, but feared breaking up their uneasy alliance.

'We can make another fifteen miles before dark,' Quinn said to Alicia's back. She shrugged, her slender shoulders moving slightly within her white blouse. Quinn tried again: 'Alicia, what you have in mind is impossible,'

'You don't care about taking the stage through to Yuma?'

'No.'

'No matter that your friend Tank Dawson asked you to do it?'

'It's impossible now.'

'You don't care about poor fat Sabato?'

'No.'

'You don't care that the murderer of my sister will ride free? About the effort your friend Mike Hancock made to see that the killer would be brought to justice?'

'Alicia,' Quinn said, spreading his hands, 'I might care. I do care about some of this, but there are many men back there who would shoot us down.' More quietly he added, 'And I care about getting you home safely.'

'Without honor?' she snapped.

'There is nothing to be done, frustrating as that might be.'

'Then do not go to sleep, Quinn,' she said darkly. 'For the moment that you do, I am taking your pistol and riding back to Soledad on my own. I swear it!'

The silver half-moon was rising as they approached the dark and silent Pueblo Soledad. They saw no bandits on the streets. There were no sounds except for the faintly ticking clock of mortality in Tom Quinn's head.

Madness.

Quinn had not been able to dissuade the

woman. He had spent half of the evening trying. Although his arguments against the wild venture were more logical than hers, nothing could weaken the woman's resolve. She had her mission; it must be accomplished or shame would haunt the rest of her years. She would not let Jody Short escape retribution. He had killed Dolores; he must pay for his crime. Her thinking went no farther. She was implacable.

Which left Tom Quinn with only two options – send the girl off to be killed by herself or go along and have both of them killed. He relished neither choice. His dilemma was somewhat akin to Alicia's. That is, he could give her the pistol and ride away from her now, back toward his ranch along the Yavapai to resume his life of peaceful contentment, but he would remain haunted as well. Never knowing what had happened to Alicia, whether he was right to abandon her in her time of need.

Quinn was no romantic, and the project was scented with doom. He turned his logic this way and that, looked down into Alicia's dark eyes as hope colored them and the suffused light of dusk flushed her face. When he spoke it was not exactly a growl, but it was close:

'All right, then. Let's get going.'

Back to Soledad as night settled and the stars flared silver-bright against a cobalt desert sky. Quinn had no doubt that they could sneak back into the pueblo. The question was, what they were to do once they had made it that far?

Alicia had her own ideas.

'I think we will capture Jody Short and tie him up. We will throw him into the stage and after we free George Sabato we will take the coach back along the road we followed down here, then strike out for Yuma where the injustices will be corrected.'

'That's a fine plan,' Quinn muttered. 'What do we do about the outlaws?'

'You have the pistol,' Alicia said with a saucy shake of her head.

'I don't have enough bullets even if every man I shot went down with one bullet.'

She was beyond pragmatism. 'Then we will have to get more bullets, or more guns.' She glanced at Quinn in the purple light of settling night. 'Unless you just want to shoot Jody Short for me and we ride away real quick.'

'No. I'm not an executioner,' Quinn answered glumly.

'It's for the best – my plan. That way you can fulfill the vow you made to Mike Hancock and Tank Dawson.'

'I made no vows.'

'And my way, Jody Short can be legally hanged. No one can ever say you were a vigilante,' Alicia added triumphantly.

As night settled and they rode on Quinn felt nothing like a vigilante, nothing like a man honoring his vows. He felt like a damn fool.

He was still trying to figure out how the woman had persuaded him to follow her into madness when they came within sight of Pueblo Soledad. There were still lights on in most of the windows, and from uptown, in which must have been some sort of cantina, came the strains of music and now and then of breaking glass.

'We'll have to wait,' Quinn said, drawing up the gray horse he was riding. 'If this is to have even the tiniest chance of success, we'll have to wait until the men are asleep. The best thing for us to do is to bed down ourselves for a while.'

'I'm too excited to sleep,' Alicia said, swinging down from the buckskin horse which had belonged to Jody Short.

'Do what you like,' Quinn said with a yawn,

untying the saddle blanket which Mike Hancock had used for warmth on innumerable desert nights. Quinn doubted that he would be able to sleep himself, but it was not because of the sort of feral excitement Alicia seemed to be feeling, but out of plain honest fear.

He stretched out on the rocky ground, thinking that by now he should have been back home on the Yavapai in his cabin. He would have left the front door open so that the breeze off the pine-clad hills could cool the room, carrying the scent of the tall trees. He would have had a roof over his head, and when he awoke, one of the ranch hands would have coffee boiling. The sun would be bright, the day full of promise.

Just now Quinn wasn't sure he would live to see another sunrise.

Sometime after midnight Alicia nudged him awake with the toe of her small boot and Quinn sat up from the rough ground, trying to remember for a minute where he was and why. The moon showed only as faint glow below the eastern horizon. The stars had grown brighter in a sky as black as pitch.

'Didn't you sleep at all?' Quinn asked.

'I told you I was excited. Excited to finish this. I

watched the town lights go off one by one. Now it is dark across Soledad. Time for us to begin our work.'

'Look, Alicia . . .' Quinn began, intending to take one more shot at trying to make her see sense, but she was not listening.

'Get up,' she said. 'I have already saddled your horse for you.

Now as they approached the town with the silver half-moon at their backs, Quinn's regret at being manipulated deepened. Alicia was smiling, her eyes eager. She was a beautiful young thing, to be sure, but he could not have let himself be charmed so easily into this ride toward perdition by a lovely smile and sleek figure. Could he? Was it her talk of debts owed and of honor? Unlikely.

More likely he was just born a fool.

'We don't even know where to look for Jody Short,' Quinn said as they paused not far from the town limits to try to formulate a crude plan of action.

'He is the new man. The prob—'

'The probationer,' Quinn provided.

'Yes, that,' Alicia said. 'They will not have given him an essential job. Perhaps they have not yet entrusted him with a gun. I believe he can be in only a few places – returned to the little room where we were kept, where Sabato is. Or,' she was thoughtful, biting at her full lower lip, 'they might have given him a simple task. To watch the horses in the stable, maybe so that no one could steal the horse-thieves' horses.'

'It could be,' Quinn answered. He preferred her first idea. If he were Guerrero, he would not leave the wanted man in custody of the horses. Jody Short would be just as likely to slip one free and risk the desert on his own. After all, he owed Guerrero no allegiance.

Quinn said in a low, uneasy voice, 'We'll try the little hotel first.'

'Good. Then we can capture Jody Short and release George Sabato at once.' Quinn just studied her wordlessly. He wondered if her eternal optimism was congenital. Or pathological.

Quinn reached behind his back now and withdrew the Colt revolver that had belonged to Mike Hancock. Deadly as the .44 was, under these circumstances it seemed a pitifully futile implement. There were at least a dozen armed men in the town. Alicia touched his wrist and said in the darkness:

'If you are forced to fight, remember to save one

94

bullet for Jody Short.'

Quinn nodded, not giving voice to the harsh response he was thinking. She probably would not have heard his words anyway. It's difficult to talk to a madwoman.

What did that make him, he wondered? He, after all, understood the dangers ahead and was hardly filled with over-confidence, and yet he rode on. They circled the pueblo widely. Quinn had never discovered whether there was a back door to the hotel where they had been kept, although it seemed there must have been. If for nothing more than deliveries, for a place to throw out slop and dirty water from the kitchen. He hoped to find such an entrance. Riding down the town's main street, even if every man in the pueblo was asleep, was dangerous business. An outlaw must be alert to stirrings even in his sleep if he is to remain alive. And the clopping of an approaching horse's hoofs is one sound they are particularly attuned to.

Riding through the scattered shade of a group of cottonwood trees behind the town they came upon a corral containing at least fifty horses. 'Well, well,' Quinn said to himself, although it should have been no surprise since a major part of Guerrero's criminal enterprise was based on horse-stealing. He drew his gray up and pondered the situation as the horses in the corral watched with interest, their curious eyes star-bright.

'It would help if we could scatter them,' Quinn said. Not only would it leave some of the bandits without mounts, the confused tracks would help to conceal their own hoofprints. 'But it has to be done in dead silence.'

'How?' Alicia asked, her voice now taut with excitement.

Quinn took a long minute to answer as his eyes studied the shadows, looking for a guard. Maybe Guerrero's men had grown complacent, lackadaisical. Maybe they never posted a guard out here, far away from civilization. Maybe the guard was drunk or asleep. No matter. Quinn had made up his mind.

'We'll open the gate. We try not try to frighten them or scatter them, just to allow them to wander out. A few of them will likely follow our own horses. Maybe the others will simply disperse.'

'I can do that,' Alicia whispered, 'while you go get Jody Short.'

The woman had incredible, baseless faith in him, it seemed.

Quinn had no better scheme to counter with.

He did not like the idea of leaving Alicia alone out here, but she was more likely to survive if caught than he was. Her father's vengeance was still a threat hanging over Guerrero's head.

Quinn glanced toward the silent town, seeing not a single lantern lit. It was very late now. 'All right,' he agreed at last. 'But you must do it silently!'

'I move like a cat!' she answered with a smile. 'I will meet you at the stable so that we can take the stagecoach.'

Quinn again swallowed the few words he would like to have spoken and walked his horse onward, toward the rear of the hotel. He was gripping the revolver in his hand so tightly that his palm was perspiring. He wiped it on the leg of his jeans, and continued.

The hotel, as he had suspected, did indeed have a back door. Not only that, it appeared by the faint light of the rising moon and stars to be standing ajar! That troubled him a little. Why would the door be left carelessly open if the adobe still held prisoners? He soon discovered the answer.

He swung down from his horse's back and approached the door, keeping his back near to the wall of the building. Three steps nearer and he would have walked directly into the man who now emerged from the hotel to stretch his arms and gaze briefly skyward. Knowing that this was his best chance, Quinn did not hesitate.

He was launching himself toward the bandit even before the guard heard the sound of footsteps and dropped his hand in the direction of his holster. Quinn had his Colt in his hand and he put a halt to the man's intention by cracking the barrel of the big blue-steel revolver across the outlaw's wrist. Thankfully, the man did not cry out, but he dropped his own pistol, half-bending over to clutch his damaged wrist. Angered now, the Guerrero man swung a fist wildly at Quinn, but Tom had been expecting it. He ducked, braced himself and slammed his forearm across the bridge of the outlaw's nose.

The guard went down as if pole-axed.

Tom stood, breathing raggedly from the exertion and the residue of peril. He bent over, catching his wind again. Then he heard the sounds of approaching horses and he crouched, raising his pistol. He recognized the new arrival.

Alicia shook her head vigorously. She was leading her own horse and Quinn's toward him. Behind her were half a dozen ponies which had followed her from the corral. An exasperated Quinn whispered at her:

'What are you doing? You said we would meet at the stable.'

'I wondered if you needed help,' she said softly.

'Get over to it,' Quinn ordered. 'We can't change out plans now.'

Alicia nodded, handed the reins of the big gray horse to Quinn and wandered off to circle the town toward the back of the stable where the coach was being stored. The stray horses scattered, some pausing to graze, a few following after Alicia on the buckskin, a couple of them wandering away aimlessly.

Quinn entered the hotel.

He held his pistol high, the barrel of the Colt beside his ear. If there had been one guard, could there be two? Or three? He toed the door open wider and slipped through into the interior of what seemed to be an unfinished kitchen. Beyond that he saw only faint light glowing, a lantern turned very low so that the wick sputtered. He entered the room cautiously and he oriented himself.

On the same bunk as he had occupied the night before George Sabato slept, apparently peacefully.

Beyond him was the slender form of Jody Short, also asleep. Glancing toward the front door of the hotel, aware that the guard he had left in the back might come to at any moment, Quinn moved swiftly.

Jody Short was jarred awake by the cold nudging of the muzzle of a Colt .44 against his throat. 'What. . . ?' he began and the pistol jammed against his throat even more roughly. 'One more word,' Quinn warned him, 'and it will be your last.'

George Sabato was now stirring. Quinn lifted a boot to shake the prison official's bed, rousing him. 'Get up now and do it silently,' Quinn commanded, and the sleep-dazed Sabato, understanding that something important was happening, got to his feet.

'What is it?' Sabato asked in a whisper. Quinn told the fat man: 'Take your belt and Short's and bind his ankles and wrists. Use his bandanna for a gag. We're leaving Soledad.'

Or so Quinn hoped. It was all up to the gods of the desert now.

SEVEN

Rather than try to carry the struggling Jody Short or make him walk, Quinn threw the killer over the saddle of the gray horse. Gagged, Short could not scream out the oaths he was trying to voice, but his eyes were filled with savage curses. Sabato was an odd combination of fear and hopefulness as he led the horse away. After taking a moment to check on the dazed guard who still had not awakened, and to slip the pistol from his inert hand, Quinn followed. Still, in the dead of night they were forced to be prudent enough to circle the entire town, avoiding Soledad's main street.

There were dozens of sleeping guns they could not risk awakening.

The stable was deserted when they arrived, except for Alicia who walked up to Quinn with triumphant eyes. 'I knew you could do it!' she said sparing a hateful glance for the bound and gagged Jody Short.

'I'm happy that one of us had faith in me,' Quinn said without much humor. He nodded toward the stagecoach. 'Let's get Short inside that thing. What are we going to do about harnessing the four-horse team? Sabato?'

The pudgy man shrugged. 'Not my specialty,' he said. He was moving toward the boot of the stage. His primary concern was obviously still the gold. Quinn grabbed his arm, halting him.

'Either it's still there or it isn't. If it's not, there's nothing we can do about it. Here,' he handed Sabato the fallen guard's pistol. 'Stand watch out front.'

Not that that would do much good. If a shooting match started, none of them would have a chance.

Quinn muscled Jody Short up into the coach and felt no pity as the killer fell on his face against the floor. Quinn closed the stage door softly behind him.

'Someone ought to keep an eye on him,' he said, running his finger through his dark hair. He was surprised to find it damp with perspiration. 'But the horses. . . .'

'I am very good at harnessing a two-horse team,' Alicia said quite calmly. 'This might take me longer, but I can do it. I will call you if I need your help. You watch my sister's murderer.'

Quinn nodded mutely. He was dead tired, more from the tension of excitement than anything else. He stood by the stage door, his eyes on Short. At the front door to the stable George Sabato stood, arms folded, Colt in his hand. If anything the prison officer looked calmer than Quinn felt. For Quinn still felt – knew – that this was madness!

They could not slip quietly out of town with the stagecoach. The guard at the hotel was bound to come to soon and raise the alarm. They could not hope to outrun a contingent of mounted bandits on the open desert.

Madness.

It was more than remarkable, it was extraordinary but they managed to get the horses hitched and the stagecoach rolling in the hour before dawn. Perhaps it wasn't that much of a miracle, Quinn reflected as he smoothly but silently started the team northward, toward the Yuma trail. Who among Guerrero's band of outlaws could have expected them to risk sneaking back into town? Their greatest aid in this mad excursion was the fact that the knocked-out guard had apparently not come to his senses yet. Quinn wondered briefly whether he had injured the man more seriously than he had intended, but did not take the time to dwell on that consideration.

They rolled silently along the trail. The hubs of the stage's axles had been well greased at Las Palmas. Quinn used neither whip nor shouts to hurry his team. For a mile or so a few of the liberated horses from Guerrero's holding pen had followed along with their herding instinct, but they soon became wary of the dry, grassless prospect of the desert flats and turned back. Quinn liked the thought of the open desert no better. Come daylight they would be exposed and vulnerable. A party of fast-riding bandits could easily catch up with them. Guerrero's last words to him echoed in his mind as he guided the team northward:

Do not disappoint me, Quinn.

Well, he had. How angry would Guerrero be, thinking that Quinn and Alicia could pinpoint his hideout for the authorities? Maybe he would decide to cut his losses and move to somewhere other than Soledad and set up a new outlaw camp. Maybe he would be so angry or determined to prove a point to his own renegades that he would hunt Quinn and the others down and punish them to the extreme.

George Sabato rode uncomfortably and anxiously beside Quinn in the wagon box. Their total armament was two handguns which would be useless should half a dozen bandits armed with long rifles come upon them.

Alicia, who had pleaded for one of the handguns, sat inside of the coach with Jody Short.

'I will need a pistol,' was what she had said. 'Then if he makes a move, I can shoot him.'

Alicia's temper was a little too hot yet at her sister's murderer for Quinn to have risked that even had they a spare pistol, which they did not.

'Just watch him,' he had said as calmly as possible. 'He's trussed, and I doubt he can wriggle free. If there's trouble we'll stop the coach and be there in seconds.'

'I would rather have a pistol,' the girl had answered stubbornly.

No, she could not have one, Quinn told her as he helped her to board the stage. Her full lips were sulky, her eyes glaring as they fixed on Jody Short. She was an angry woman. But surprisingly she paused before the coach door was shut, bent low and kissed Quinn again. Another of those innocent, butterfly-light kisses before her savage mood returned and she sat in the seat opposite Jody Short, her arms folded beneath her breasts and glared at him with consuming fire in her eyes.

'What do you think, Quinn?' George Sabato was asking now as the first hint of gray dawn streaked the eastern horizon. 'Will we make it?'

'I have no idea,' Tom answered honestly. 'I don't even know if this is the right trail.' For Paco had known the road well enough, having traveled it many times, but to Quinn it was just a wandering thread across the trackless desert. 'All I do know,' he said, guiding the plodding horse team on, 'is that come daylight we had better be alert for any sort of trouble.'

'I know Guerrero might be coming,' Sabato snapped as if Quinn had taken him for an idiot.

'Yes,' Quinn said quietly, glancing toward the prison officer. 'And I hope you haven't forgotten that there are Apaches around.'

Sabato seemed to shudder a little, but he said nothing in response. He obviously had not forgotten the earlier raid. Still, despite their lack of weapons and precarious position, Quinn believed that Sabato would stand in a fight. He must have seen a lot of trouble in his twenty-three years as a prison guard.

'I still wonder about the gold,' George Sabato said.

'Yes, but I told you earlier—'

'I know,' Sabato said sharply. 'It's there still or it's not. We can't do anything about it either way.'

'That's right.'

'We could stop and I could take a quick look,' Sabato suggested hopefully.

'Do you really want me to halt this coach right now?' Quinn asked, glancing eastward toward the lightening skies.

'No. I suppose not,' the chubby man answered after a moment. 'It's just that – Quinn, you don't understand that my reputation, my career are dependent on delivering that gold to Yuma Prison.'

'You don't understand,' Quinn muttered, 'that if we don't keep this stage rolling, neither you nor the gold has a chance of ever making Yuma.'

Sabato held any retort he might have made and the stage swayed and rumbled on across the long white desert.

Alicia had removed Jody Short's gag because the young outlaw was having trouble breathing.

No shouts for help could now do him any good.

Besides, she wanted to talk to him, to ask him why. Why had he done what he did to Dolores Delgado? She put it to him bluntly:

'How could you kill my sister like that? She was a good woman.'

'Who says I did it?' Jody Short snarled, rubbing his throat. Wearing that gag had been nearly enough to strangle him.

'The jury did. I do,' Alicia said with venom. 'You did not know that I saw you that day, but I did. I was right behind Dolores on the trail.'

'You're mistaken,' Jody tried.

'I am not!' Alicia said to the beady-eyed bandit. 'The jury was not mistaken. Your face had scratches on it from her fingernails. Your horse's hoofprints were found at the scene. A piece of your shirt was clutched in Dolores' hand. That is why I did not come forward. It was not necessary then. If they had found you innocent then my father would have let me testify. There is no doubt that you committed the crime, Short. I just need to know why.'

'What does it matter to you?' Short demanded. He lifted his hands which were still bound with his own belt.

'It matters.'

Jody Short's face contorted. His Adam's apple bobbed in his throat. His feral eyes met Alicia's and he shouted:

'Because she was dirty! All women are dirty. They try to hide beneath their finery, their skirts and stockings, but they are dirty things! I would like to kill them all.'

Alicia just sat staring at the young man for a long time. Short had been twisted inside somewhere in his life. She couldn't guess and didn't care to know what might have perverted him. She only knew that she had been right – Jody Short must be executed. The stagecoach jolted on across the desert.

'Somebody's on our backtrail,' George Sabato said to Quinn. Glancing across his shoulder, Tom Quinn also saw the distant rider illuminated by starlight.

'Doesn't take too much to figure who it is,' Tom muttered.

'Can't you get some more speed out of these animals?' Sabato asked worriedly.

'They're giving it all they've got. Truth is they could use a rest about now.'

'I thought you said that you scattered all of their

horses,' Sabato said, clinging to the iron seat rail as they hit a deep rut in the road.

'Those that we found,' Quinn answered, 'but those probably weren't even their personal mounts. Besides, most of the horses could have been easily caught up again.'

Sabato was still studying the backtrail. 'I can only make out one rider,' he said with puzzlement. 'That makes no sense, does it?'

Quinn didn't bother to answer. Nothing that was happening on this tangled journey made a lot of sense to him.

A quarter of a mile farther on the lone rider, who was obviously gaining ground on them, could be more clearly seen, illuminated by pale light in the eastern skies.

'Quinn,' Sabato said, 'pull the team up – it's the woman who's trying to catch us.'

'Lily Davenport?' Tom asked in disbelief.

'Yes. I can recognize her now.'

'Damn all,' Quinn said, drawing back on the reins to slow the team. 'Now we're in for it.'

Because even if Guerrero was willing to let them escape into the desert, knowing that they now knew the location of his hideout, he would not be so willing to let his lover escape.

Quinn reined the team to a full stop. The horses blew and shook their heads with relief. Lily Davenport drew up beside them minutes later on a frothing black pony. The horse's eyes were wild; hers were no tamer.

'Thank God!' she said. Her body was shuddering. Alicia leaned halfway out of the stagecoach window to gape at her.

Quinn was laconic: 'Short honeymoon.'

'I didn't know . . . I have to go with you. I think my horse is injured,' Lily said in between gasps.

There was no time for debate. Tom just told her, 'Make it quick!'

Lily, showing she had some heart, quickly unsaddled the black horse and slipped its bridle before turning it free to make its way homeward. She climbed aboard and Quinn snapped his reins. The coach started on its lonesome way again.

'Was that smart?' George Sabato asked.

'I don't know, Sabato. I'm not sure I've done anything smart for the last few days. It's done, that's all.' He shrugged and returned his attention to guiding the team along the barely visible trail across the trackless, dimly lighted desert.

For hours they continued across the deceptively desolate land. Empty and lifeless, it seemed, and

111

the skies held clear, but there were hunters out there, and the sudden thunder of guns hung only briefly in abeyance.

Quinn knew all of this, yet the constant strain of holding the four horses on to their path, the battering his body had taken in Las Palmas still bothering him, his concern about Alicia, forced him to focus only on the task at hand and leave the watching and worrying to George Sabato.

'Shouldn't we have reached the road to Yuma by now?' Sabato asked anxiously.

'I don't know.'

'Maybe we passed it by! How long did it take us when that man, Paco, drove us to Soledad?'

'I can't recall.'

'If we miss the coach road, we're doomed, you know that, don't you?' Sabato asked.

Probably. Quinn was starting to believe that they were doomed anyway. He was weary, his shoulder joints feeling as if they had been separated by the constant tug of the reins. His back hurt, his legs ached from the beating he had taken in Las Palmas. He was driving a weary team across a featureless desert. The sun would rise soon and grow white-hot as it arced into the skies, and then they would find themselves waterless beneath its glare and, if lost, quite definitely doomed on the desert flats.

There was nothing for it. Quinn did not think he could have missed the Yuma coach road, but in the darkness of the previous night, it was possible that he had. He thought that Sabato was right about one thing – it had not taken the coach this long rolling south from the road with Paco driving to reach Soledad. Or had it? He cuffed cold perspiration from his forehead. His body clock did not seem to be functioning well. Surely they would hit the stage road soon? Had to. Even with a weary team, the going would be easier on it than it was through this sand.

And there was the chance that they might encounter other traffic on the main road. A stage going in the other direction, freighters, even an army patrol. They had to find the road to Yuma.

Then it suddenly seemed that it no longer mattered if they did or did not.

'They're coming, Quinn,' Sabato said. 'Half a dozen riders, maybe more, on our backtrail. It looks like we've had it.'

EIGHT

It seemed that Sabato's assessment of the situation was correct – they had had it. But Quinn was not going to make it easy for Ernesto Guerrero's raiders. He drew up the team as the faintest dawn color limned the eastern horizon and ordered Sabato:

'Give me your pistol.'

'What? You'd leave me unarmed!' Sabato replied in shocked disbelief.

'You're driving now. I have already proved to myself that it's impossible to drive a team of four and shoot at once.'

'I can't handle the team!' Sabato objected. 'I've never even attempted it.'

'You'll have to now,' Quinn said, handing

114

Sabato the handful of reins, eight in all. He showed Sabato how to place the leather ribbons between his fingers. The fat man continued to shake his head.

'I can't do it, I tell you.'

'You can get them started. That's all that's necessary for now. Give me that pistol.'

'What are you going to do?' Sabato asked, his voice quavering. He handed Quinn the pistol which Tom shoved down in front, behind his belt, thinking irrelevantly that the world owed a debt to the man who had invented holsters.

'I'm going to climb down and make it a little harder on them,' Quinn replied as he prepared to swing out of the box. 'It's the woman Guerrero's after, of course, but we can't surrender her. They probably would not let us go on to Yuma anyway, knowing what we do.'

'I don't like this,' Sabato complained.

'Nor do I,' Quinn said

He swung easily to the sandy earth and walked to the coach door. Peering in at the unhappy Jody Short, at Lily Davenport and Alicia, he told them, 'Sabato's going to drive. I'm going to stay and try to hold the outlaws back. There may be a chance if Sabato can cut the stage trail.'

'You haven't got a chance, Quinn,' Jody Short growled.

'Probably not. But the rest of you might. If I am successful, Lily and Alicia might be spared – and you, Short, might yet survive long enough to meet the hangman.'

Short just glared at him. Lily Davenport hung her head. Alicia rose with determination.

'I am staying with you,' she announced.

'Oh, no, you're not,' Quinn replied strongly.

'Yes, I am. You have two weapons, I see. I am a good shot.'

'No,' Quinn said flatly. Alicia was trying to push past him to exit the coach.

'I am a determined woman,' she said.

'I'm starting to get that idea,' Quinn said. Still he barred her way.

'You can't stop me. I will simply jump out when the coach starts again and make my way back,' Alicia told him.

'What the hell is the matter with you?' Quinn asked the crazy woman with the black eyes.

'You shouldn't have to stand and fight these men alone, and there is no one else to help you,' Alicia said.

There was no point in arguing further. The

approaching riders were much nearer now, the dust rising from their horses' hoofs showing as a sheer veil against the pink of the dawn light. Quinn backed away and let Alicia leap from the stage, handing her one of the pistols without comment. He returned briefly to look up at George Sabato who sat as if paralyzed on the box of the coach.

'Let them run,' was the best advice Quinn could give the prison officer, 'if disaster threatens, just pull back on all eight ribbons as hard as you can.'

'Quinn . . .' Sabato began in a pleading tone.

Tom Quinn took his hand and slapped the near horse on the rump with all the force he could muster and the stage lurched into uncontrolled motion. The last thing he saw by the pale light of new dawn was George Sabato's bloodless face, his eyes wild with panic as the four horses lunged forward across the desert.

'He was frightened,' Alicia said at his shoulder as they watched the dust settle.

'So am I,' Quinn told her. 'Let's find a place to set up our ambush.'

As they slipped from the road into a shallow wash where some greasewood and a few huge stands of nopal cactus grew, Quinn asked Alicia:

'Did Lily tell you what happened back there? Why she made her escape?'

'She said,' Alicia answered, panting, grabbing at Quinn's supporting arm as they slid down the quartz-sand bank, 'that she heard Guerrero, Rafael, the blond man, Lon and some of the others discussing business when they thought she was asleep. The talk was of 'eliminating' some of their competition among the border raiders. They might have even been talking about my father,' she shrugged as they climbed back up the sand bluff to search for concealment, 'but there was murder afoot – that was made clear. And Guerrero told the others that if you and I broke our promise to him – that we would be eliminated as well.'

'She must have known what sort of man Guerrero was,' Quinn said, tugging Alicia down beside him as he bellied up to the rim of the wash.

'When she met him, he was handsome, dashing, quick of wit, easy with a smile. She swears she did not know,' Alicia answered as the following riders now drew out of the dawn shadows to become distinct figures. 'Sometimes a woman in love sees only her dreams, and not the reality of the man.'

Quinn was listening, but not paying a lot of attention to the dark-eyed girl. He sighed heavily,

118

drew back the hammer of his big Colt and waited, watching the coming horsemen. He could hear Alicia's rapid shallow breathing as she lay beside him, the blue-steel pistol looking huge in her small hand.

'Don't fire until I do,' he told her, 'or until they start it.'

They had a total of twelve bullets against an enemy with hundreds of rounds of ammunition at their disposal. Whatever they accomplished it would have to be economically and quickly done. Quinn's original idea had been simply to hold Guerrero back until the stage carrying the women could reach the coach road then try to make a run for it himself as best he could. That might or might not have been foolish, even suicidal, but he couldn't see the women taken again by the border raiders.

Now with Alicia remaining stubbornly behind with him, he knew there would be no chance of the two of them making a dash for freedom.

He would just have to see to it that Guerrero changed his mind about the wisdom of tracking that stagecoach down.

They had several small advantages over the border bandits. They had surprise on their side.

They were in a concealed position. The bandits would have to fire from horseback – always a chancy proposition.

'Don't use all of your bullets in the first volley,' Quinn said in a whisper. Alicia nodded mutely.

For Quinn, although he had only six shots, he meant to waste one firing into the ground in front of the Guerrero raiders' horses. That would give the bandits pause to consider and slow them down. The problem with that idea was that alert eyes could spot the smoke rising from his pistol and pinpoint their position. Yet Quinn had an inborn prejudice against shooting down even men like these from ambush. There was also the slender chance that they could talk their way out of this. Guerrero had led his men out in a rage, no doubt. Maybe his ardor, the eagerness of his men had cooled somewhat after the long ride. Perhaps knowing that they had ridden into a fight they had not expected would instill caution.

Thinking through all of that as the horsemen approached, Quinn knew that none of his speculation was useful, that they were a collection of vague hopes and wishful thinking. He tried to pick out Guerrero among the riders, for if all else failed, he meant to take out the leader of the border raiders first, hoping that the rest would scatter in confusion.

The raiders were nearer now, much nearer. Quinn was able to identify Guerrero riding near the front of the pack. Hatless, he wore a white shirt and black trousers. Beside him rode the blond kid, Lon. The fat man, Rafael, did not appear to be among them.

'Here goes,' Quinn said raising his sights toward the path of the horses. 'If the shooting starts, don't spare a man— or a horse if that's the only shot you get. And. . . .'

'I know, don't use every bullet in the first salvo,' Alicia said with a snappishness caused by tension.

'That's right,' Quinn said. For if any of the Guerrero men swung down and rushed them, they would have to be ready to take them down at close range.

Quinn fired his warning shot.

And everything that could go wrong did.

This was no rabble riding after them. All of them were experienced fighting men and instead of drawing their horses up they scattered in every direction, unlimbering their guns. Quinn winged his second shot at Guerrero, but missed as the outlaws began to fire back. Quinn saw Alicia unleash a bullet from her .44. Her shot struck a border raider's buckskin horse and it went down, but the rider leaped free, the only noticeable damage a limp as he raced toward cover. Three shots out of twelve gone, and nothing to show for it.

Tom fired again. His shot might or might not have hit Lon. It was difficult to be sure because the bandit went to the side of his horse and rode on, Indian-style. A dozen bullets from the outlaw guns sprayed the earth just above their heads as Alicia and Quinn ducked low.

'They've spotted us for sure. We've got to move,' Quinn shouted.

'Where?' Alicia asked, searching the dry wash behind them.

It was a fair question. There was little brush in the draw. Only some flimsy greasewood and the clumps of nopal cactus. He inclined his head and nodded toward the cactus thicket. Alicia's eyes widened. Even if they could make it that far, the result was bound to be painful. And the paddle-shaped blades of the nopal weren't going to stop any bullets aimed their way. Quinn saw no other choice. At least the cactus would offer concealment. Perhaps Guerrero would decide to forget them and continue his quest for the stagecoach. More likely, Tom thought grimly, the bandit chief would simply split his force, leaving a few riflemen behind to take care of them.

There was time for a spasm of regret at having gotten Alicia into this, but no time to dwell on it. They slid down the flank of the gully in whirls of dust, hit the flat ground and raced for the cactus patch. A bullet whispered past, much too near, as they ran on. Once the other bandits had figured out where they were going, every man on the rim above would open up with his weapon and they would have no chance after that.

Quinn's mouth was dry, his heart pounding, his breathing ragged as they reached the half-acre-sized stand of nopal. There were game paths through the head-high cactus where a few browsing animals had passed and smaller creatures had come to hide or to retreat from the heat of day.

'Get down and get in there,' Quinn said, half-pushing Alicia to her hands and knees. Almost immediately she suffered needle-like punctures on the palms of her hands. Quinn heard her cry out in pain, but he pushed her ahead as he scooted into the thicket. There was no way to avoid the thorns and their bite was brutally painful, but Quinn kept on, urging Alicia ahead. The stinging of the cactus needles was far preferable to the angry bite of a .44 slug.

They made their way to a sort of clearing in the stand: ten feet or so of naked ground where some animals had apparently made their bed. The cactus loomed high on every side. They could see the blue sky only in patches. Alicia was biting at a thorn in her hand, trying to remove it with her teeth. Quinn didn't take the time to remove the spines he had piercing his own hide. He sat cross-legged watching the entrance to the thicket for any man daring enough to follow them. None would be eager to attempt it, he thought, and the next minutes proved him correct. The gunmen started to fire their weapons into the big thicket. They had no visible targets and the cactus-stand's size offered too many possible places of concealment. Still, several bullets penetrated their shelter, ripping through the fibrous paddles of the cactus. Quinn put his arm around Alicia and forced her to the ground to lie beside him.

'I just got most of the stickers out,' she complained but not bitterly. The ground, too, was strewn with thorns and she had collected many other piercing barbs as she was pressed to earth.

'What are we going to do, Quinn?' she asked, looking up at him with understandable fear in her eyes.

'They can't keep the shooting up for ever. They must know it's just a waste of ammunition – and I don't think they're likely to try to burrow in after us. We wait,' he said. 'They'll give it up sooner or later. They have to.'

'How will we even know if they're gone?' Alicia asked logically.

'If we must, we'll wait until dark and try it then.'

'Spend an entire day in this horrible place?' Alicia asked. It was already dreadfully hot on the desert, and every small movement carried the risk of new puncture wounds. The ones they had gotten earlier were already beginning to fester and itch. Quinn did not answer. He had no answer. They would remain in hiding like quivering rabbits. It seemed to be their only chance of escaping alive.

An hour passed in slow torment. Once a rattlesnake slithered past, but they ignored one another and it went about its own business.

'Do you think they've gone?' Alicia asked hopefully, but the words had no sooner passed her lips than a barrage of rifle fire sounded again from the opposite bank. Timing the shots mentally, counting them, Quinn took it for two men with repeating rifles.

'I think Guerrero's gone. He's left a couple of men to keep us pinned down until he can return.'

'With the coach? With Lily?'

'That seems to be his idea,' Tom answered.

'What will he do after that? What would you do, Tom?'

He shook his head. He didn't wish to answer her. He knew what he would do if he were Guerrero and it scared the hell out of him. The nopal would not burn, but that did not mean that by collecting litter and dry brush a fire could not be started. If he were Guerrero, had the time and enough anger in him, he would try to smoke them out of the thicket, leaving them with the choice of asphyxiating or emerging to take a bullet. Tom did not know what choice he would make in that eventuality.

'Can we surrender?' Alicia asked at one point as the day grew drier, the air in the thicket more stifling.

'We'd end up right back where we started,' Tom reminded her. 'If we were that lucky.'

Alicia was as aware of that as Quinn was. She also knew that this time Ernesto Guerrero would not even attempt to play gracious host. She was starting to get more uncomfortable with each passing minute, unable to rise, unable to even shift position without new pain. Her suggestion had been only grasping at straws.

It was dusk before Quinn could dredge up the nerve to try it again. The day had been long, sweltering. They had had no food, no water. The cactus spines were a constant torment. But with death waiting beyond the thicket, there had been no choice but to remain where they were. All of his thoughts were fixed only on keeping Alicia alive now. The stagecoach and its passengers meant nothing at the moment, not Sabato's gold, Jody Short's date with the hangman in Yuma, nor the careless Lily Davenport.

Only Alicia. And the small woman was exhausted, suffering mightily. He touched her arm and said, 'Come on. I think they're all gone,' breaking the silence they had held as the hours of deprivation had passed. 'I'm getting you out of here.'

'Can you, Tom Quinn?' she asked with the

127

weakest of smiles. More roughly, he said:

'Come on.'

Carefully, then, they again made their way on hands and knees across the blanket of thorns, the cactus around seeming to lash out at them in their passing. The sky beyond held a purple haze. A dry wind had risen with the sundown. That brought a small bit of relief. It was enough to nudge their spirits slightly higher.

At the exit to the thicket, Quinn held Alicia back with his arm as he studied the opposite rim of the wash. He could make out no silhouettes of man or horse. That did not mean that no one was there, but he had hopes that he and Alicia would be as difficult to spot from that side of the gully as the Guerrero riders were from theirs. They were now risking bullets, but it seemed to both of them to be preferable to smothering to death in the thorny thicket.

'Which way?' Alicia asked, remaining in a crouch as they emerged.

'Not downhill, that's for sure,' Quinn answered quietly, his right hand tight around the butt of his Colt revolver. 'Up and over, out of this gully.'

Alicia only nodded obediently. She could have asked him a dozen questions, such as where they were to go if they did manage to get out of the wash, which direction would they strike out in, how could they hope to find water. She said nothing. She touched his shoulder briefly, lifted sundown eyes to his and nodded. She would follow wherever he led.

Moving slowly, keeping their silhouettes low, they circled the stand of nopal, climbing over rocky ground now. Alicia slipped once, banging her knee roughly, but she stifled her cry of pain. Quinn tugged her to her feet and they started on as the last glow of color flushed the western sky with crimson and gold. They were a dozen steps away from the rocky rim when the man with the gun appeared, back-lighted by the sundown skies.

'Hold it right there, Quinn,' he commanded. 'Or I'll gun you both down, the lady first.'

NINE

Lon wasn't kidding, Quinn knew. The blond-haired gunman stood, legs spread wide apart, revolver steady in his hand, staring down at them with expressionless eyes.

'Looks like the game is over, Quinn. Why don't you make it easier on all of us and drop those guns?'

Lon was a dark silhouette against the lurid backdrop of the sundown sky. Quinn considered trying to take him, but he was on uneven ground; the gunhand was ready. And he remembered Lon's words. The man was without mercy; undoubtedly he would keep his threat to shoot Alicia first.

Quinn let his pistol drop from his hand. Not

fighting back did allow Alicia a slender chance of surviving this night, depending on Guerrero's mood. She glanced at Quinn unhappily but not accusingly and let her own pistol fall to the rocky earth. Lon backed away from the rim of the gully and gestured with the barrel of his revolver.

'All right now,' he said with grim satisfaction. 'Clamber up here.'

Quinn led the way up the sand and rock of the bluff. Alicia, following, slipped and went to hands and knees, a small cry escaping her lips. She was exhausted, water-deprived, her hand and knees pierced by thorns. Quinn slid back down to help her to rise. Guiding her by the elbow they made their way to where Lon stood. The gunman did not seem amused, nor was he triumphant. There was no expression at all in his eyes or on his stony face.

'What now?' Quinn asked, his chest heaving with the exertion. Alicia was tilted against him for support.

'I wouldn't know,' Lon said between thin lips. 'Personally I couldn't care less about you two, but Guerrero might have something in mind.'

'Such as?'

'You'd have to ask him,' Lon said without concern. 'There's a place not far along here where

131

the bluff has broken down. We can cross the wash there. That's how I got up here. But let's get going before darkness settles.' Now Lon did look slightly uneasy. It was the falling night, Quinn realized. The night into which Lon had sent so many of his enemies.

He feared that long night as well.

'Let's get moving,' the blond gunman ordered, motioning with his pistol. It was then that the rifles from the far side of the wash opened up. Five, six or more. Lon halted, glanced that way and while he was distracted Quinn threw himself against the gunfighter. They fell in a jumble to the rock-strewn earth. Quinn had struck Lon on the neck just below the ear as they fell; now, on top of him on the ground, he winged wild rights and lefts at the bandit. He used no science, only ferocious instincts. Quinn was a wild thing trying to fight for his life and protect his woman.

Lon fought back furiously, like a cornered wildcat, using knees and elbows, fists and skull. But Quinn's first savage blows had taken some of the steam out of the badman's blows. Exhausted as he was, Quinn was still the bigger man and he had his adversary pinned. One thudding right landed at the hinge of Lon's jaw. Quinn felt the blow send tremors from his wrist to his shoulder as it struck. Lon felt nothing. He lay sprawled and unconscious against the desert.

The rifle fire still racketed across the gorge. Now and then in the dusk muzzle flashes could be seen as Quinn got slowly, heavily to his feet, snatched up Lon's handgun and walked to Alicia who had seated herself on the ground and seemed unable to rise.

'Are you all right?' Quinn asked crouching down beside her in the near-darkness.

'Who is shooting, Quinn?'

'I don't know,' he had to admit, shaking his head heavily. 'But you and I have to get away from here. Can you walk?'

'Yes, of course I can,' she said with injured pride. But as Quinn helped her to her feet again, she wobbled and swayed in his arms. She could not go on now. Not without rest, without water. But they had to move away from the area. With the pistol in one hand he stooped, scooped Alicia into his arms and began making his trudging way north. Alicia struggled at first, tried to argue, but she didn't have it in her. It was amazing how light she was, even as debilitated as Quinn himself felt. They went on as darkness invaded the desert skies.

A hundred yards on the horsemen halted their progress.

With Alicia in his arms, Quinn did not even consider trying to bring the Colt revolver into play. Two men, each with unsheathed rifles, sat like black silhouettes against the last remnant of burnt orange color offered by the dying sun, blocking their way. This was it then. The end of the long trail which led nowhere.

'What are you doing?' one of the men demanded loudly.

'Just . . . trying to get . . . home,' Quinn said with immense effort.

'Put the girl down,' he was ordered, 'and don't think of trying to use that pistol. You would have no chance.'

That was so. Quinn let Alicia slide slowly to her feet. The Colt remained gripped in his hand. He did not mean to surrender it – his only tenuous tether to survival.

'Toss them your canteen, Luis. They need water.'

Quinn frowned, not understanding at all. The man next addressed Alicia.

'Are you all right, girl?'

'Yes, Father, thank you.'

'Luis, send someone back to take care of that,' he said with a disparaging glance at the still unconscious Lou.

The rifle fire had died down. Crossing the gully again, Alicia behind her father on his strapping black horse, Quinn mounted behind the silent Luis, they reached a rough camp and they paused to sit on the still-heated earth on a spread blanket and drink the blessed tepid water from canteens.

Vicente Delgado had shed his sombrero and rolled a cigarette. The smoke was bitter-smelling, but not unpleasant as it rose in layers into the warm desert night.

'Can you tell us what happened?' Quinn asked.

'Only this,' Delgado answered. 'The eastbound stage reached Las Palmas yesterday and the driver told Aaron Pyle that the westbound coach had never reached Yuma and he had not passed it along the road. I was notified, of course.' Quinn nodded, not knowing why 'of course'. Apparently Delgado had much overt or covert power in Las Palmas.

Delgado continued. His hooded eyes showed only a calmness that he could not have felt when the news of his daughter's abduction had reached him. 'I turned this matter over in my mind,'

Delgado was saying. His hand now rested on Alicia's shoulder. 'Who would have taken a stagecoach away? For what reason? Highwaymen, bandits might have taken what money or jewels they could steal and ridden away, but a stagecoach! It would only slow them down as they tried to elude the law.

'More, who was capable of this act? It would have to be a well-organized gang with a place near enough to the border that they could escape to and feel safe from pursuit. I then thought of my old ... amigo,' Vicente said the word harshly, 'Ernesto Guerrero.'

'He had a hideout not far south of the stage road. In Soledad. I knew that he had faithful men around him, a large profitable enterprise based there. I still could not reason out why Guerrero would want a stagecoach, but in my mind I was nearly certain that it must be him who took it. I summoned twenty men and we rode to Soledad.

'The stage was gone when we reached the village. Ernesto was gone, but I found a man I knew,' Delgado said thinly, 'a fat little man named Rafael. You might have met him. I offered him – incentives – to tell me what had happened.

'Within the hour we were on the trail

northward. We caught up with Guerrero and his men just as they had managed to halt a stagecoach with a foundering team pulling it. They fled as they saw us. Guerrero knew it was no good to try lying to me as he has so frequently in the past. I looked first into the coach, but Alicia was not there. Only a taffy-eyed woman with brown hair, a little crazy-looking man with his hands bound.

'We pursued Guerrero again. Not far from here he decided to make his stand. You must have heard the fight. He knew that the vengeance I would extract would be far more painful than any a bullet could offer.

'The man was many things, but not a coward. The fight was brief but bitter.

'And now,' Delgado said, 'as you can see, Guerrero is not here and I am.'

The story, long as it was, still left much to the imagination, but the finer points did not concern Tom Quinn just then. He was dog-tired, yet his body tissues were slowly absorbing the water he had been drinking, and settling night brought some small relief from the heat of day. He felt that he had to go on.

'You say the coach horses had been run into the ground. Did you see the driver?' Quinn asked.

'The team stood trembling, heads hanging. They had had no water and had been run hard,' Delgado answered. 'As for a driver, I did not see one. Only the bound man and the woman with the taffy eyes.'

'You left them there?' Alicia asked, not totally surprised.

'Was I to bring them along in pursuit of Guerrero, into the teeth of a gun battle?' Delgado said with a short laugh.

'No,' Alicia said, 'but—'

'I tossed them a canteen. I did not free the bound man although he begged me to.'

'I have to catch up with them,' Quinn said, rising. His own legs were unsteady now.

Vicente Delgado's dark eyes only watched, expressing nothing. 'Do what you must,' he said coolly.

'Can I get a horse?' Tom asked.

'Guerrero's men left many,' Delgado said without humor. 'Take your pick.'

'Pick out two of the freshest ones, Tom,' Alicia said and now she too struggled to her feet.

'He doesn't need two horses,' Vicente Delgado commented.

'Of course he does,' Alicia said. 'Am I to walk?'

138

'You are continuing – to Yuma?' her father asked without apparent surprise, but with concern.

'It is what I started out to do,' she answered with a toss of her head. 'It is what I promised my sister.'

'She is stubborn, no?' Delgado said to Quinn.

'She is stubborn,' Tom agreed. 'Would you be willing to accompany us along the trail – in case some of Guerrero's men are still lurking?'

'It is not good for me to stay north of the border for too long,' Delgado answered. He did not explain. Tom thought that he needed no explanation to understand. 'After this is over, Quinn, will you bring my daughter home?'

Quinn hesitated in answering and Alicia replied forcefully before he could. 'I will not be coming home, Father. I am going to live up along the Yavapai. With Tom Quinn.'

'I see,' Delgado mused.

'Do you object, Father?'

'Not if it is a thing done under the laws of God.' He rose then and shook hands with Tom Quinn, who stood dumbstruck, frowning deeply. 'Good luck to you both,' Delgado said. Tom started to speak again but Vicente Delgado told him: 'Say nothing. It is pointless. The girl will have her way.'

Tom had plenty to say, but he did not feel like

going into it then, not with Alicia's father present, so he just accepted the premature congratulations mutely. Delgado beckoned his aide, Luis, and gave him a series of orders in rapid Spanish.

'Horses will be brought to you and a waterbag. Is there anything else you require?'

'Is there any chance that someone has found a spare holster?' Tom asked. He had been carrying his pistols behind his belt for days now and his flesh there was rubbed raw, front and back.

The horses that were brought looked relatively fresh. Tom recognized neither of them – a stubby little pinto pony and a long-legged gray. Alicia did not waste a lot of time in goodbyes. She hugged her father once, whispered a word or two into his ear and then swung aboard the pinto. The silver moon was rising to their right when they again started up the trail, and the grooves the wagon wheels had left in the sand were easy to follow by its light. A coyote crossed their trail, looked up with annoyed surprise and darted into the gully.

'You are not speaking,' Alicia commented another mile on. 'Are you angry with me?'

'How are you feeling?' Quinn asked.

'Not so bad,' she shrugged, 'I have a lot of itching all over from the cactus. You did not

140

answer my question. Are you angry with me? Is it because of what I told my father?'

'It's usual for people to have an understanding between them before a marriage is announced,' Tom said grouchily.

'I thought of that before I spoke – but I had to tell my father. Who knows when, if ever, I will see him again? I did not want him to worry.'

'So you didn't mean it?' Tom asked, puzzled by the girl.

'Of course I meant it,' she said with surprise. 'I am a determined woman. You, Tom, you are a stubborn man or else you would not still be at this task. Therefore, if we both set our sights on the same target, there is nothing that can ever stop us.'

Tom shook his head. That was a sort of logic, he supposed, but not the sort he was used to. The moon cast shadows across the sand and back-lighted Alicia. Her profile was beautiful in moonlight and after another mile or so, he forgot his anger.

'What do you think we will find when we reach the coach?' Alicia asked.

'I have no idea. Horses dead in their harnesses? George Sabato trying to walk out of the desert – he might have taken the gold and made an attempt.

He feels that strongly about his obligation.'

'What about Lily Davenport? And Jody Short?' she asked, speaking his name as if it left a foul taste in her mouth.

'We can hope for the best,' he told her. 'We won't know until we catch up with them.'

'Guerrero's men – do you really think there might be some of them still around?'

'Not if they've got any sense,' was Tom's answer.

The night wore on; the moon as small and bright as a silver dollar rode high in the sky.

'I can see the rabbit,' Alicia said to herself as she gazed skyward.

'What rabbit?' Tom asked in bafflement.

'On the moon.' She pointed skyward. 'You have to look at it just right and you can see the rabbit on its face.'

Tom glanced that way, shrugged and put his mind on other things. Like the missing stagecoach, like the dangerous Jody Short, who might somehow have managed to free himself in their absence, like the 'taffy-eyed' Lily Davenport, who would not be safe if the little killer decided that she was 'dirty' as well.

'Now can you see it?' Alicia asked with a child's delight.

Let her have her rabbit on the moon. Quinn was more concerned with the coyotes on the desert.

It was only an hour or so before dawn when they eventually came upon the stagecoach.

Amid all the long-spreading desolate silence of the vast desert, it appeared more desolate and silent than the land itself. Quinn held up his hand and they halted, sitting their horses side by side on the low sandy knoll overlooking the flat where the unmoving stage rested.

'Could they all be asleep?' Alicia asked in a low, taut voice. Tom did not answer. He loosened his Colt in its holster and they started their horses on again.

Riding slowly toward the moon-shadowed stage they saw no sign of movement, heard no voices. The desert whispered against itself. Therefore it was all the more startling when the man rose from behind a stand of creosote brush and called out:

'You there! Rein in – I'm coming out.'

TEN

Quinn's hand had dropped to his holster. If this was one of Guerrero's bandits, he was ready to shoot it out with the man, little as he liked the prospect. But it was not. Staggering across the sand, a heavy canvas sack across his shoulder, came George Sabato, appearing shrunken, utterly weary.

'I thought it was you, Quinn,' Sabato said as he reached the horses. He looked up pleadingly. 'Have you any water?'

Alicia untied the three-gallon burlap water bag from her saddle pommel and passed it to him. Delgado drank greedily, lowered the bag and drank again. At last he wiped his hand across his mouth and handed the heavy bag clumsily up to Quinn, who asked:

'What are you doing out here alone, Sabato?'

'Hiding the gold from the bandits,' he said gesturing toward the now-familiar leather-handled bag lying at his feet. 'I haven't come this far just to lose it now.'

'What happened?' Quinn asked.

'The horses couldn't run anymore, and the raiders caught up with us. Then a second band of men arrived. There was a lot of shooting,' Sabato said. 'When I could, I slipped to the rear of the coach and recovered the gold. I made it into that stand of brush and stayed there all day, never knowing who would come back or when.'

'What about Jody Short?' Alicia demanded.

'And Lily,' Quinn asked.

'I saw no more of them,' Sabato answered. 'I didn't know what was happening, but if the stagecoach was their target, I wasn't going to remain there with the gold. My career depends—'

Quinn interrupted him. He had heard all of that before. 'Climb up behind me. We have to get back to the coach. We have reason to believe that the fighting is all over now.'

Sabato did not argue. He seemed unconvinced, but he was too weary to refuse. Heavy canvas sack still in hand, he swung up behind Quinn on the

145

gray horse, and they continued on their way across the moon silvered desert.

Dawn was nearing, but it was still dark as they approached the stagecoach, darker now that the moon was heeling over behind the western mountains. Quinn rode with his pistol in his hand. He did not like the eerie silence. Someone should have heard them coming and emerged from the coach. Unless they weren't able to. Sabato slipped awkwardly from the back of the horse and Quinn swung down, approaching the coach in a crouch, the Colt cool in his hand. He took a quick peek inside, lifted his eyes just above the window sill, then holstered his weapon, shrugging. 'They're gone.'

'You mean that Jody Short got away?' Alicia said, rushing to join him. 'How could he?' She swung open the door to the stage and peered in as if Quinn had made a mistake, as if Short and Lily Davenport had somehow hidden from him. 'How could he?' she repeated. The straps that had bound him lay on the floor of the coach.

'At a guess,' Quinn said, 'I'd say that Short convinced her that they were now alone on the desert, and she would need his help to get out alive. She would have set him free if she believed

146

that. Alone, frightened with Guerrero and another bunch of gunmen around, she might have seen freeing Short as her only chance to survive. He would have had hours to convince her as the night rolled past and no one came to her rescue. He must also have reminded her of the near-meeting with the Apaches.

'Frightened enough, she might have done that.'

'Where could they be?' Alicia asked, searching the long desert with her eyes. It had grown cool as morning approached. She had her arms crossed beneath her breasts and her teeth chattered just a little.

'They could be anywhere!' Sabato said. He was frantic, but not over the missing passengers. His gold was all that was important to him. 'We've got to get going again,' he complained to Quinn.

'Yes, we have to,' Tom told him. 'First, though, we have to find Short and Lily.'

'But why. . . ?'

Alicia told him in a scolding voice:

'Because you do not know the little man as we do. He is capable of any act. Do you want to wash your hands of any fate that might befall Lily Davenport.'

'She's the reason we're in this mess,' George

Sabato replied.

'Yes! And is that a reason to leave her in the desert with a woman killer?'

'I guess not,' a shamed Sabato said. 'What do you want to do then, Quinn?'

'You still have your hat,' Quinn said with seeming irrelevance. Sabato frowned in confusion but did not respond, waiting for Quinn to continue. 'We have almost three gallons of water in that bag. Give each of the horses a drink out of your hat. If it looks like any of them is absolutely incapable of continuing, we'll cut them out of the harnesses and make our way as best we can. But it's cooler now. They've had a long rest. With water they might be able to take us as far as Yuma if we take it easy on them. If we have to, we can try putting our saddle horses into harness, but that is an uncertain prospect at best. Let the horses drink, and we'll see what condition they're in when we're ready to roll on.'

'All right,' Sabato agreed. 'What are you going to do, Quinn?'

'What do you think? I am going to find Lily Davenport.'

'I'll go with you,' Alicia said quickly. He did not try to argue her out of the idea. He knew her well enough by now to know that it would have been useless anyhow. 'How do we proceed?'

'There's still enough moonlight for us to be able to see their footprints. There will be a lot of hoofprints from the bandits' horses, but these will be overlaid on them. One set will be of a man's boots, the others will be much smaller.' Alicia gave him a half-mocking little smile as if he were stating the obvious.

Quinn went on, 'Since the last place Jody Short wants to end up is in Yuma, and we know they wouldn't want to go south toward Soledad again, we'll try north and east first.'

'I'll look to the east,' Alicia said.

'Very well, I'll try north. Try not to get out of sight of the coach,' Quinn said severely. 'I won't have you lost out here.'

'Because you do care?' she asked hopefully. Quinn grunted a response which was no answer.

'Don't mount until you have found something. It's much more difficult from horseback, even for experienced trackers, and neither of us is that. If you find their tracks just call out. There's no need for silence. Anyone nearby will already know that we are here.'

They spread out then, leaving Sabato to water

the horses. Methodically Quinn walked on, leading his horse, searching the sandy earth for tell-tale signs. He was more concerned for Lily than he had let on. True, she had gotten them all into this situation, but he still believed her to be more naïve than cunning. No matter which, she did not deserve to fall victim to the ruthless little maniac, Jody Short.

The moon was fading rapidly. Quinn still had not been able to cut their sign and now the dim afterglow he had been working by was nearly gone. Neither had Alicia had any luck. He could see her distantly criss-crossing the desert, searching for boot prints. Perhaps they were doomed to fail despite their good intentions. The entire run had been a disaster from the first moments; why should he hope that his luck would change now?

The sand underfoot was deep, deep enough for any impressions to have remained. There had been no noticeable wind blowing to drift the sand over their tracks. Quinn was beginning to wonder whether he had not guessed wrong again. Many things could have happened: for example one of the killed or injured raiders might have left his horse behind. Short and Lily Davenport could have caught it up and now be miles away on its back.

Quinn halted, gripping the reins to the gray horse tightly.

From somewhere a small sound had reached his ears. Soft, somehow pathetic like the mewling of a lost kitten. It came again. Ignoring his own advice, he swung into leather and started the long-legged horse in the direction of the sound.

A few hundred yards on he halted the gray, patted its neck, listened again, and the sound came to him once more. Now he was sure – it was a human voice. He heeled the big horse roughly toward its source.

He did not have to travel far. Arriving at the rim of a shallow wash, he saw her immediately. Lily Davenport lay on her back, skirt pulled nearly up over her head. She was thrashing and twisting. Her voice was muted because Jody Short, hair hanging in his face, had his hand over her mouth. Quinn started his horse, changed his mind and dismounted on the run. He half-slid, half-fell, down the sandy slope and charged Short full-bore, lowering his shoulder as he collided with the demented little man and drove him from Lily's body.

Short came to his feet with a savage hiss, his fists bunched. His eyes lit with apparent delight as he recognized Quinn. He wanted to kill someone, it seemed. Anyone, so he lunged at Tom. It was a futile and brief murderous tantrum, for Quinn unholstered his Colt and clubbed Jody Short above the ear, putting all of his strength into the blow. Short fell face forward into the sand and lay there, his body twitching spasmodically.

'Did you kill him?' Lily asked, sitting up with effort.

Quinn had been trying to determine that. He rolled Short over and examined his victim. Short's eyes were rolled back into his skull, but he was still breathing. 'He'll live long enough to hang,' was Quinn's assessment. He rose, dusting his hands and holstered his Colt.

'Are you all right?' Tom asked Lily Davenport.

'I suppose so. I've been foolish all my life, but this is as close to losing my life over foolishness as I ever hope to come. I can't thank you enough. This is the second time you've saved my life, Quinn.'

He felt like telling her that it was time for her to find a way of saving herself from herself but held his tongue.

Now behind them, Quinn heard a horse descending the sandy bluff in a flurry of dust.

Alicia drew up her wild-eyed pinto pony and rushed to him, 'Tom!' she said, sparing Lily only a single unreadable glance. She almost hugged Tom Quinn, but not quite. She halted in her tracks and stood hovering over Jody Short with poison in her eyes.

'Give me your pistol, Tom!' she said.

'No.'

'I want him dead.'

'I know you do. But we haven't come this far only to have you do murder. He will be executed. By other hands, not yours.'

The daughter of an outlaw, Alicia had grown up learning a different code of justice. This was the man who had killed her sister, Dolores. He deserved to die, and it was her responsibility to see that he did. Tom Quinn walked to her, rested his hand on her shoulder and spoke softly.

'It is for others to do, Alicia. Not for you. You would never feel clean afterward.'

Now she did throw her arms around him and hug him, her eyes streaming tears. He could feel her trembling in his embrace, but the quaking did not last long. After a moment she drew away from him, wiped her eyes and nodded.

'Sabato will be wondering what's become of us.'

153

And so he was. By the time the four of them reached the coach again, with Jody Short's hands tied behind his back with Quinn's bandanna, the fat prison courier was nearly at his wits' end. His face brightened as he saw Quinn, Jody Short riding in front of him, Lily Davenport riding behind Alicia, clinging weakly to her, approaching.

'Thank God,' Sabato said. 'I was wondering if the Indians got you.'

Lily slid unsteadily to the ground. Jody was unsaddled roughly. He cursed as he was led to the coach, telling everyone that he had done nothing to Lily, 'But I should have! She's as dirty as the rest of them.'

Lily, briefly clinging to Quinn's arm, asked in a low voice, 'May I ride up in the box with you? I can't stand to look at that insect for another minute.'

That was the way they made their way to Yuma: Quinn driving the team which, though exhausted and stumbling, nevertheless had recovered enough to make their plodding way, Lily Davenport on the box beside Quinn. George Sabato rode in the coach opposite Jody Short who railed against all womankind for a few miles and then lapsed into a dark silence. Alicia rode

154

alongside on the pinto horse. The gray had been tethered on behind.

The weary miles passed with excruciating slowness. The red sun rose at their backs. Yuma, squat, little city that it was, rose from the desert before their eyes. By eight a.m. they were settled and safe, prisoner and horses led away to their final destinations, the team to much-deserved fresh water and oats, Jody Short to his tiny cell on death row.

Fed, rested and in clean clothes, they walked out of the small hotel that afternoon. Some sort of report had to be filed with the stage company, something must be said to the local sheriff. They would withhold certain bits of information, of course. Nothing could be said about Vicente Delgado's involvement in the affair.

The day was dry and windless. Almost immediately they met George Sabato, his pink face newly shaven, his suit brushed, striding toward them. The little man was beaming. 'They welcomed me as a sort of wandering hero,' he told Alicia and Quinn as they stood together in the band of narrow shade cast by a storefront awning. 'I managed to bring the gold through after an Indian attack and an ambush laid by border raiders. And I brought Jody Short in. Quinn . . .' he said uncertainly, 'you won't tell them that I was not nearly as brave as they seem to think?'

'No. What would that profit anybody?' Tom answered. Let Sabato have his moment of glory, it cost Tom Quinn nothing.

They talked to the sheriff, who took in their tale with only occasional indications of disbelief. At the end of it the man, who shared his regret at the fate of Mike Hancock, rose from behind his desk and shook hands with Tom.

'There are a few discrepancies between what you have told me and what George Sabato says, Quinn. But none of that matters. All I know is that you did us a service in bringing the stage through to Yuma with all the passengers safe aboard.

'I meant to mention this to you – do you remember the three men who assaulted you in Las Palmas?'

'Of course,' Tom said bittterly.

'It seems that they have been identified. Two brothers and a cousin. The cousin was out of a job and hoped to get work driving the Yuma coach after he heard the regular driver had been killed.'

'That was the reason they were trying to run me off? So that he could have the job?' Quinn almost laughed. If it hadn't been for his perverse nature, after the beating the men had given him he would gladly have stepped aside in Las Palmas. All the man had to do was ask for the job.

'Is that settled, then?' the sheriff asked.

'I suppose so,' Tom said. 'Though if I ever see those men again . . .' he glanced at Alicia, small and hopeful as she stood beside him, 'I'd like to thank them.'

'I don't get you,' the sheriff said, shaking his head as he walked them to the door of his office, 'but no matter, you came through like a champion on your first run.'

Tom halted, turned back to face the lawman, and then smiled thinly. 'That wasn't my first run, Sheriff. It was my last run.'

Back at the hotel, they took the time to eat again in the dining room. Across the room, they saw Lily Davenport in close conversation with a man they had never seen. He appeared tall, strong and a little arrogant. Well, maybe she had found her hero this time.

'While you were washing up,' Quinn told Alicia, 'I ran into Sabato again. No appeal was filed for Jody Short. The execution is in the morning. Sabato has fixed it so that you can be there.'

'No,' Alicia said with surprising softness. Her eyes were turned down, her lips only slightly parted. 'I do not wish to go to it. I know that this is the reason for my long journey, but I have decided, Tom Quinn – I have decided that from now on I will celebrate life and not death.'

'I think it's healthier,' Quinn commented. Their coffee was arriving and they removed their hands which had been touching each other's from the table so that the waitress could serve them. When the woman was gone, Alicia requested:

'Tell me again about the Yavapai range, Tom.'

He shrugged with one shoulder. 'There's not a lot to tell, really. It's at altitude high enough so that pine tees grow there. I have a small creek running practically past the front door of my little cabin. It's peaceful, quiet, a lot cooler than it is down here on the flats. It's not much to look at, I suppose, but it suits me.'

'Then,' Alicia said, again reaching across the table to take both his hands, 'it will suit me as well.'